Ad Asylum

Ad Asylum

DAN WALD

iUniverse, Inc.
New York   Bloomington

iUniverse books may be ordered through booksellers or by contacting:

iUniverse
1663 Liberty Drive
Bloomington, IN 47403
www.iuniverse.com
1-800-Authors (1-800-288-4677)

Because of the dynamic nature of the Internet, any Web addresses or
links contained in this book may have changed since publication and may
no longer be valid. The views expressed in this work are solely those of
the author and do not necessarily reflect the views of the publisher, and
the publisher hereby disclaims any responsibility for them.

ISBN: 978-1-4401-8284-6 (sc)
ISBN: 978-1-4401-8285-3 (ebook)

Printed in the United States of America

iUniverse rev. date: 11/18/09

Pitch Minus 11 Days—Sunday

I'm watching my poor cell phone. I think it's become schizophrenic. I've programmed it with so many different ringtones for so many different things that it's lost its identity. One tone for my clients, one for my boss, one for my work friends, another for my creative director. Then there's the buzz for when I get e-mails, another buzz for text messages, and of course another one for incoming Tweets. Sometimes three different incoming transmissions hit at once, and the poor thing just kind of has a seizure. The most pathetic thing is when it's on vibrate and I've put it down on a table or something—it sort of flails around like a bug on its back on a hot sidewalk. I think it may actually be trying to kill itself. I swear it's trying to get to the edge so it can jump off and put itself out of its misery.

I'm sitting inside my cubicle watching my phone's attempted suicide so I don't stare too hard at Rachel. I hate it when she catches me staring. She's off-limits. She has rules. But she's practically sitting on my lap at my desk and opening the files from the flash drive she just inserted into my computer. It's Sunday afternoon and the place is deserted, otherwise we wouldn't dare look at what she's about to show me right here in my cubicle. They're the initial ideas for the upcoming Leary pitch, which is completely hush-hush.

She opens the files and clicks around to show me the concepts. I'm dumbstruck by how bad they are.

"These are horrible! I mean they really, truly, god-awfully suck! Please tell me you're kidding. You're kidding, right? I'm getting punk'd, right?"

Rachel just shakes her head. "I know. I'm embarrassed to be working on this."

It is now, right here and now, that the conspiracy is formed. Our own secret plan to save the venerable thirty-year-old agency that provides us with meager paychecks, emotional abuse, and fourteen-hour days. No words are exchanged, but we both know. We aren't going down without a fight.

Let me back up.

Our employer, Halliday and Vine, is in the midst of a major pitch for the mother lode of accounts—one of the biggest pitches likely to come up in what has been a dismal year. We're talking over $150 million in global billings. More importantly, it is our chance to redeem ourselves after losing two big pitches in the last quarter, not to mention an airline client that went bankrupt and a banking client where the CEO and CFO were both recently indicted.

But this is all common knowledge. What is less known is that two other large accounts are teetering on the brink. Duke Owen Pollard, our master at IMH, the holding company in Paris, is ready to unleash the hounds of hell upon us should we screw this one up.

And it is clearly ours to lose. Our CEO and half namesake, Jack Halliday, went to college with Mitchell Leary, the philandering founder of House of Leary, the multibillion-dollar eight-hundred-pound gorilla of the fashion world. When Mitchell sneezes, underfed models around the world catch cold. Boutiques on Rodeo Drive and factories in China hold their breath. And the bitchy editrex of the fashion magazines scramble to provide $200 handkerchiefs.

House of Leary has decided after decades with the same agency that it is time to take a "fresh look." Everything is of course all air kissy kissy and "You're welcome to join the review," but the writing is on the wall for the incumbent agency. (Their office furniture is already for sale on eBay.) Sales are sliding and the once-impregnable brands of H of L are beginning to seem old and shabby against the popping-up-like-Whac-A-Mole designs of hip-hop artists, rappers, tattooed convicts, and American Idol winners.

And the reputation of Halliday & Vine, until recently that is, has been that of brilliantly unconventional, creative approaches. So this pitch should have fallen right into our sweet spot. But that was before the untimely disappearance of Peter Vine, the other half of our letterhead, who delved deep into his own psychosis to create ads that truly stunned and amazed. He went off his medication, and suffice it to say that his dramatic and very public demise was not a pretty scene. He's been missing ever since.

We all figured that our current chief creative officer, Drew Reed, must have graphic video tapes of both Jack Halliday and Duke Owen in order to keep his job. Saying he is a dullard is an insult to dullards. But he defines the agency political operative. He can send you to agency purgatory with a single look, e-mail, text message, IM, or Tweet. He cares more about power than creative. And he is an absolute master at leaving others holding the bag — he has fall guys all lined up for his scapegoats. Worst of all, he has one of those little sorta-goatee things hanging under his lip, and he always dresses in black and talks with a fake British accent.

Which brings me back to what Rachel has just risked life and limb to show me—the initial creative concepts for the pitch. I truly hope that this is a joke, but the look on her face tells me it isn't.

We're down on my floor because it's too dangerous for me up on the creative floors, even on a Sunday. It's basically open season on account people up there. We're the enemy, plain and simple, despite all the efforts at integrated teams and information sharing. The silos are worse than ever, even after years and years of trying to break them down.

And now, on top of the age-old tensions between the Account, Creative, and Media departments, each agency has piled on Interactive, Experiential, Mobile, and something called Social Networks, each with a team of "experts" vying for client budget dollars, awards, prestige, power, resources, and hair gel.

Yup, we're just one big, happy family.

And that brings me to yours truly, Ryan Simmons. I'm the account exec, or AE, on the world's second-largest dandruff shampoo account. An AE is the lowest of the low—worm food, pond scum, tooth fuzz, absolute dog crap. And best of all, we do all the work and take all the shit. The only ones who treat us worse than our clients are our own colleagues. I spend the bulk of my day lying to my client, begging my fellow agency "teammates" for the stuff they owe me, and being yelled at by the media people and ridiculed by the creatives.

And I fought to get this job. I was one of ten interns who worked here for free for two summers during college only to find out that only two of us would be hired upon graduation. At a sub-sub survival salary. I have three roommates, 2,587 if you count the roaches and mice. My subway commute to the outer reaches of Brooklyn takes me an hour each way.

I started in research. Spent two years trying to make sense of focus groups and consumer research reports so that our creative gods can base their ideas on actual consumer data. I'm not sure they even read it. The better ones do, but most of them get their ideas when they're drunk out of their minds or naked in the shower.

The fun part is then watching them fall in love with their ideas regardless of their merit. Better yet is when they die on a sword to defend them. This of course gives them an excuse for at least a week of pouting and hissy fits, not to mention an inability to get any other work done.

Which means that I'm coming up with yet more excuses for my client as to why their storyboards for yet another exciting dandruff shampoo commercial are late.

But back to the pitch ideas. My BFF Rachel has shared the ideas with me because I'm the only one out of nine hundred employees that she likes and trusts. As a peon graphic designer, it was totally random that she got onto the pitch team. She had been on the aforementioned banking account, and instead of getting fired, she was put on the new business team, as she can keep her mouth shut and do much of the scut work required.

Rachel closes the files on my desktop and takes out the flash drive.

"Let's go get drunk."

*   *

Rachel lives in the complete opposite direction from me, way uptown on the West Side, so we go around the corner to the agency's favorite watering hole, affectionately called Ar, as the B in Old Towne Bar has been broken for as long as we've been coming here. The Old Towne Bar is a fairly typical midtown bar-pub thing. The menu is the same as bar-pub things everywhere. The smell is somewhere between frat house, grease, and cigarette smoke that still lingers although smoking in bars was banned years ago.

To those of us who work at H&V, Ar is as much a part of H&V as Halliday and Vine themselves. It's the place where agency victories are toasted and losses drowned. It's the first stop for those who get laid off—a pink slip is worth a free drink—and the lunch spot of choice to welcome new employees. Glance around the walls and you'll see the entire history of H&V's most famous campaigns in framed pictures dating back thirty years.

Jimmy, the bartender, sees us coming in. I give him a slight nod to acknowledge that we'll both have the usual, and we head toward the far end of the long wooden bar to our favorite stools. Jimmy is combination hippie, Vietnam vet, and biker—leather or denim vest, ponytail, varying facial hair, and a few tattoos just visible on his arms when he wears a T-shirt.

It's somewhat empty at six o'clock on a Sunday night. We check to make sure that no one from H&V is around. All clear. Jimmy deftly places a margarita in front of Rachel and a perfectly poured draft Stella in front of me. Rachel starts right in.

"Drew is such an absolute dickweed."

I sorta grunt, as I'm watching Rachel lick some of the salt off the rim of her margarita glass. Her tongue is somewhat of a sight to behold.

Perhaps I should explain Rachel. She's very hard to put into a box, especially as all of the descriptive boxes have disappeared by this early part of the twenty-first century. First off, by any standard measure, she's hot. She's twenty-five to my twenty-six. Her hair changes often in color, style, and length. Right now it's short, maybe sorta retro punk, kinda deep reddish brownish. Her body has caused pileups, and she dresses to tease, but in a way that is never slutty or too obvious. I don't know how she does it. Even other women tend to like her, lust after her, or both. But it's impossible to dislike her.

The only thing I don't like about her is that she has a rule: she doesn't date guys she works with, period.

She's also wicked talented, but to date that's been completely lost on Drew and the other powers that be in the illustrious creative department at H&V. She can draw and conceptualize like you wouldn't believe. Graduated top honors from Parsons and has a killer book. Hopefully one day she'll graduate from doing layouts and type treatments, but for now she understands that she has to do her time like the rest of us peons.

"You realize that if we don't win this account, we're going down."

"You mean we can't survive on dandruff? I happen to be doing a phenomenal job. Just ask my client. She loves me."

"That's great, Ry, but it's only three million in billings."

"Yes, but imagine what the world would be like without it."

"Okay. Your life has meaning. Can we move on?"

"Sure. But only after I tell you another bitch story."

"If you must."

My client, the Flake-Off dandruff shampoo brand manager, is known simply as "the bitch." I didn't even start it. It was started by the creative director on the account five years ago and passed down like a sacred heirloom. By now she probably even knows about it. She probably likes it.

My biggest mistake was finally giving her my IM screen name. I'd managed to avoid it for months, but she persisted. And yes, I'm aware that I can make myself invisible — I'm not an idiot. But if the client wants you on IM, you have to be on IM. And you can't be hiding.

If she makes me follow her on Twitter, I will kill myself.

So now she just randomly IMs me to curse me out. Flaming e-mails no longer satisfy her need for verbal violence.

And how lucky am I that they're based in NYC so I can run over there all the time. She takes pleasure in calling meetings giving me thirty minutes notice when it's pouring, sleeting, or 95° and humid. And when she knows I don't have whatever deliverable it is she's screaming about, just so she can watch me squirm and make up lies.

She's about thirty-one, and I swear she's probably never gotten laid. She's not ugly; she could actually be attractive if she didn't wear those stupid brand manager costumes. She never got the memo that said casual dress was okay.

It's more like she has zero sensuality. You must know what I'm talking about. There are women who might not be objectively beautiful, but they're so sexy. It's how they move, it's how they smell, it's how they talk, it's how they dress. You want to jump into bed with them for the weekend and never come out.

And not only does she verbally abuse me, she comes on to me at least once a month. Forces me to have dinner with her. I've even had to travel with her to make store visits or attend focus groups, which then leads to having to fight her off late at night in the hotel bar. I've told her I'm gay. I've told her I have a girlfriend. I've told her I have a 250-pound black boyfriend. I've told her I'm impotent. I've told her I have herpes. I've told her I'm married. I've told her I have mother issues. I make her drink until she falls asleep, and then we both pretend it never happened and she starts abusing me again.

Yes, it's a wonderful life.

"She IM'd me yesterday all excited that she met some guy on eDating. Ninety-six percent compatibility."

Rachel spits out the sip of margarita she just took and almost chokes to death as she laughs hysterically.

"Pictures," she manages to blurt out. "We must have pictures."

I start laughing as well, and we both just let it go for a bit. It feels so good to just laugh out loud together like two idiots. When it finally runs its course, Jimmy arrives unbeckoned with round two, and we get back to the business at hand.

"So you really think Drew is a dickweed?"

She almost loses it again but manages to continue.

"It's amazing. He has five of our best creative teams working on this, and this is the best crap they can come up with. And all of them are too afraid to tell him that the ideas suck."

"You're not."

"Are you kidding? I can't even get near him. I actually went to his office and spoke with his assistant. When I tried to get on his calendar, all she did was laugh. She actually laughed at me and said, 'Drew doesn't meet with your kind.'"

"You could stalk him and try to speak to him."

"I tried that too. I nailed him coming out of the men's room. He looked at me and said, 'Who are you?' I told him. He looked at me with disdain, said nothing, and walked away."

"So much for the open door policy so eloquently discussed at the last agency town hall meeting."

"They're gonna blow it. Our last chance, and they're gonna blow it big-time."

"Is Chas on the pitch team?"

"Of course. Drew and Chas are attached at the hip."

I wince. Chas is the ass wipe of a creative director who works on my account. We're not exactly what I would call friends.

"We have to come up with something better."

"Thanks for that brilliant insight."

"And we have to take down Drew and Chas at the same time."

She looks at me and flashes a devilish smile.

*   *

Pitch Minus 10 Days—Monday

An ad agency on the brink exudes a tension that is palpable the moment you enter the building. You can smell it. You can feel it. You can even see it—the tight faces of those who think they're about to get fired, the scurrying about by those who are desperately trying to look busy when they have absolutely nothing to do.

And elsewhere, there's the excitement of those select individuals who are on the pitch team. They are like a crazed band of zealots who are both energized and terrified at the same time. The rest of us view them with envy, as at least they have a mission. Win or lose, they at least know which way is up.

I approach my cubical and boot up. I see Nate wandering out of the pantry with a cup of coffee. Nate and the rest of the tech guys are the only ones who drink the company coffee. The more burnt and nasty it is, the more they seem to like it. They watch the rest of us with our $4 Starbucks or Dean & Delucas and just kinda smirk.

The tech guys hate you, unless you're a hot babe or can hold your own in *World of Warcraft*. Which I can. Which is why they tolerate me. I also know as much about technology as they do, but I never admit it. But they know.

"Hey, Nate. Question for ya."

Nate is wearing his uniform—a red baseball cap, a black T-shirt with the faded graphics of an '80s metal band, ripped jeans, and old sneakers. He doesn't answer, just glances at me from under his cap with a look that says, "Don't tell me you forgot your password."

"Think you could hack into eDating?"

I actually get a smile.

"Need a date?"

"Never pay for it. I want to find out who the bitch's new boyfriend is."

Now he's really smiling. I've never seen his teeth before. I don't think I ever want to see them again.

"Pictures. We want pictures."

He wanders off muttering, "I'll see what I can do." Like everyone else, he's glad to have a mission.

I walk back to my cube. My phone message light is blinking. I've got twenty-seven new e-mails, five marked urgent. All from the bitch. My IM icon is blinking. The bitch again. And then, of course, my phone vibrates.

It's a Twitter Tweet. I've been following my ex. She's getting married. I've been following it step-by-step as some sort of primitive cleansing strategy. Like that Native American sun dance thing where you poke bones through the skin of your chest, attach them to a pole, and then walk backward until you pull them out. Pain that purifies. Or something like that.

Just left Fina with Chad. China is gorgeous gorgeous gorgeous!

I'm sure that Chad had a blast. Knowing him, he probably did. I hate them both.

I sit. I open my cheap, $1 large coffee from Momar, the vendor on the corner. Nate would be proud: it tastes like crap. I dive into my work.

For the next two hours, I lie to the bitch three different ways using four different technologies as to why the dandruff guy shots have yet to be retouched. I sweet-talk Sally, the media planner, into giving me the online budget. I spend a half hour on a conference call with the web dandruff team trying to talk them out of creating a Catch the Dandruff game. I fail. Oh well. I'm sure ten people will play it. There goes $45K down the drain.

Then my boss buzzes me. Can I come in for a minute?

I groan inwardly. My boss, Bruce, is the biggest wimp I've ever met. He's like a black hole of negative emotion. I feel like the essence of life is sucked right out of me every time I walk into his office.

"Hey, Bruce. What's up?"

He looks up from his desk and takes off his glasses like the weight of the world is resting on his shoulders. Poor Bruce handles all the crappy accounts that the agency has. A million here, three million there, two million over there. Small brands, small budgets, no glamour, no glitz, no awards. Funny, though, at this point in time, Bruce's $20 million in billings is more stable than the $40, $50, and $75 million accounts that come and go on a chief marketing officer's whim.

"I hear that the dandruff shoot went over budget. How could you let this happen?"

Oh man. I knew this was coming. Chas the ass wipe insisted on having his supposed photographer girlfriend do the shoot. The whole day was a cluster F on top of a disaster. And of course the supposed photographer girlfriend insisted on using her supposed good-looking brother as the model. The guy had such bad skin that everyone assumed we were doing an acne shoot instead of one for dandruff. Of course, his hair was perfect. Not a flake in sight.

"Yeah, we went overtime. I'll handle it."

I'll handle it by threatening Chas into threatening his girlfriend to take a lower fee. I'll steal the rest from another budget.

"You better, Ryan. I'm sick of this happening all the time. You've got to learn to keep your creative team in line, or they'll walk all over you. We've had this discussion before, haven't we?"

"Yes, Bruce. It won't happen again."

I turn to leave, but I'm not fast enough.

"Have a seat, Ryan."

Shit. Here comes a lecture on how to work with a creative team. Another half hour of my life shot to hell.

"Did I ever tell you about the time we had to do a shoot in the Mojave Desert?"

Only a million times.

"No, Bruce, I'd love to hear it."

My phone vibrates. More ex Tweets.

Oh my God, oh my God, oh my God! Daddy got our date at the country club!

*   *

Rachel stops by my cube toward the end of the day. Creatives can wander freely on our floor without fear of physical or emotional harm. Nothing like a double standard.

"Hey, Ry. So what's the plan?"

"The plan is—I have no plan."

"I thought you were an evil genius."

"When's the pitch?"

"Less than two weeks. Thursday afternoon at four o'clock. Here. The main conference room."

"Are we first, last, middle?"

"We're last. There are three pitches ahead of ours. They're doing them all in one day, starting at seven o'clock that morning."

"Is it good or bad to be last?"

"I'd say it's good. But it doesn't matter if we suck."

"True."

"So we have less than two weeks. Plus our real jobs."

"We also have no budget."

"Now that you mention it, we don't have any other people on this. Like people with real talent."

"We don't have access to the research."

"No clue on competitive analysis."

"No market data on share, or media spending."

"No war room."

"So what's the plan?"

"Bwaahahahaha! That was my evil laugh. I have no idea."

"I have an idea. Let's go shopping."

*   *

As always, Rachel is right. It's an early spring evening, and our offices are not far from the primary shopping blocks on Fifth Avenue. Not a place I venture very often.

"You, my dear, are going to get a speed education on the world of high fashion."

"I hate shopping."

"That's okay 'cause we're not shopping. We can't afford anything. We're just going looking."

We head into Bergdorf Goodman, a first for me.

The next several hours are truly eye-opening for me, a member of the great unwashed, "high end is Banana Republic" class. I've never seen *What Not to Wear*. Dressing well is so low on my priority list that it's not even on my priority list. I can't afford dry-cleaning. I wouldn't know how much to tip a shoe shine guy.

This is a whole new world.

Rachel and I wander for hours, dodging the cologne sprayers while we pretend to be spoiled rich brats from the Upper East Side.

I try on $400 shoes and feel the difference between cashmere and silk sports coats. I try on a $4,500 suit with a $300 tie and then a $2,500 overcoat.

I could get used to this.

We wander through the jewelry department, and Rachel fusses over a $15,000 necklace. The saleswoman is having an orgasm until Rachel turns up her nose and we wander away.

And I'm sucking it all in. H of L brands own the top end as well as the middle. Nothing on the lower end. Their brands are high quality, classic, like butta.

But they're certainly not cool, edgy, innovative, or hip.

Sales are declining because P. Diddy, Jay-Z, and Lil' Kim are eating their lunch. The country club crowd is still with them, but their numbers ain't going up.

I say good night to Rachel with my head spinning and my body yearning for the feel of cashmere and silk.

*   *

Pitch Minus 9 Days—Tuesday

Getting dressed this morning was extremely depressing. I've never realized how truly pathetic my wardrobe is. I'm still wearing stuff I wore in college. I wear the same shirt twice, sometimes three times before washing it. Dry-cleaning? Starched shirts? My pants haven't seen a crease for years on end. I have one suit for important meetings and two sport coats that I have no idea when or where I purchased them.

Shoes? I have a brown pair and a black pair. The brown pair has some sort of Hush Puppies–type fur. The black ones are penny loafers—$75 from L.L.Bean. I rotate them day by day with no thought whatsoever to what I'm wearing.

But I was perfectly happy in my ignorance. Now I'm ruined. Ruined, ruined ruined.

I get in early the next day and spend an hour cruising the fashion sites and glamour magazines online.

Nate wanders over.

"Hey, Ry. You know, it's kinda funny, but I don't know the bitch's real name."

I laugh out loud.

"It's Rebecca. Rebecca Pierce."

Before I can ask a question, he is gone.

It's just as well. My phone is ringing. It's the ass wipe CD's extension. I let it ring, picking up on the fifth ring.

"Ryan."

"How dare you send Amy's invoice back to me! You have a lot of nerve."

"Oh hi, Chas. And how are you this morning?"

"Cut it, Ryan. Sign off on the whole amount, or I'll make your life a living hell."

"You already make my life a living hell. You'll have to do much better than that."

"You agreed to use Amy. And you agreed to her fee."

"That was before I knew she had no talent."

"I'm warning you—"

"No, Chas, I'm warning you. You broke about ten company policies in insisting that your girlfriend get hired. I wouldn't have minded if she'd gotten the job done. But she didn't. We went over on the shoot, and now we're going over on airbrushing the goddamn zits off her stupid brother's face. So tell her to take what I'm willing to pay and send me a new invoice, or I'll just have to visit the trolls in finance and compliance."

"You're dead, Ryan."

"I'm shaking in my boots here, Chas."

He beats me to hanging up on him, but that's okay. He knows he's beat on this one. But I'll pay for it.

I'm already universally despised by the eleventh floor. I'm not sure whether to be proud of it or upset about it.

The creatives are the prima donnas of the advertising world, and we're an agency that became famous for its creative prowess. So getting hired as a creative here actually means something. Especially when Peter Vine was running the show.

Peter Vine was one of those rare gifts to the advertising world. He struggled mightily with his own demons, but he was a talented, nurturing soul who knew that the way to truly develop talent was to hire the best and protect them enough to come into their own.

There were much fewer turf battles and nary a hissy fit when he ran the show. Creatives of all types—designers, animators, musicians, copywriters, illustrators—they all flocked to H&V, and under Vine's guidance, they filled walls and walls with awards. More importantly, they drove their clients' businesses with ads that hit home or hit hard or made you laugh. And they got you to buy the product. Peter Vine knew that the awards didn't mean crap if the clients missed their sales goals.

He was one of the best. Most of his protégés have since left H&V for better opportunities.

Drew, on the other hand, attracts creative directors like Chas. Petty, untalented, overpaid whiners.

And those are their good qualities.

When Peter had to leave the agency, the place changed almost overnight. Jack Halliday was a decade older than his partner; he's now in his early sixties and no longer has the fight in him that we used to love him for. He was legendary for his standing up to both clients and our masters in Paris. He always regretted selling the agency and tried several times to buy it back. But he lost his fire when Peter was ousted.

Drew was forced upon us by Duke Owen. Drew is of the creative school that focuses as much on the bottom line as on the quality of the work. He hires suck-ups and yes-men without regard to their talent. He's penny-wise and pound-foolish.

I got along great with the creatives that were part of Vine's team. They left their egos at the door. We'd fight tooth and nail over creative directions, but they didn't hate us. We cheered our victories together and drank away our losses when the client killed good ideas.

I can already imagine Chas sitting at his desk plotting ways to screw me over on our next dandruff adventure.

My IM is flashing. I wince until I see that it's Rach257.

You've got a date 2nite. Don't make any plans.

I'm intrigued. What's her name?

Ramon.

You mean Ramona?

No, I mean Ramon. He's six foot two, and he'll kick your ass if you make a pass at him.

K then.

No questions. Meet us out front at 7:00 PM.

B.

B.

*   *

So I spend the rest of the day actually working—including the four phone calls of ten minutes each getting screamed at by Chas's girlfriend. I let her vent. It lets her express her feelings. I finally agree to cut her fee by 25 percent instead of 35 percent, and she feels like she's won. I don't tell her that I would have settled in-between.

But as hard as I'm working, I can't help but wonder what my date with Ramon is all about.

Rachel has been completely AWOL. She's not on IM, she's not answering her phone, and she hasn't replied to e-mail. I don't even know if she's joining us or not.

It's 6:45 and I'm just about to head out when my phone rings. Caller ID says it's the bitch. Crap. Do I take the call? I better. She can see that I haven't shut down yet, as I'm still on IM.

"Hello, Rebecca."

"Hey, Ryan. Do you have a minute?"

She sounds unusually contrite. This is not good. It means she wants to discuss her personal life. This could take awhile.

"For you? Of course. But I have to meet some friends out front in fifteen."

"At least you have friends."

Uh-oh.

"What's up?"

"I don't know. I just feel like such a loser sometimes. All my friends are already married and having kids, and here I am waiting around to see if some guy I don't even know on eDating will even get back to me."

"Of course he will. You're 96 percent compatible. How could he not?"

"I know, I know. I keep telling myself that. But it's been like eight hours or something."

"Oh c'mon. That's like nothing. He could be in meetings all day."

"He works from home."

"Then conference calls"

"He doesn't have two minutes to respond to my e-mail?"

"Back up, back up. Tell me how it works."

"So first I took the free compatibility test. Then they tease you and let you look at your highest matches. And there was Don at 96 percent. I thought he was cute. And he lives in Philly, so it's not like he's across the country. So I joined a few days ago and contacted him.

"And you heard back?"

"Yeah, right away."

"So he was interested. He was psyched."

"Totally. We exchanged IM addresses and IM'd for like two hours."

"So what was your e-mail?"

"Well, I sort of suggested that maybe we get together."

"So now you think you spooked him?"

"Yeah. Maybe I seemed too desperate."

"I think you're good. He's already seen your picture. He IM'd with you for hours. You hit it off. Now, he's just maybe trying to play it cool."

Tick. Tick. Tick. It's 6:53. I gotta get off this call.

"Oh, oh my God! There's his response! Oh my God. I'm scared to open it. Gotta go, bye."

She hangs up. I promise myself that I'll light incense, bow to Mecca, and slaughter a goat tonight in hopes that good ol' Don sweeps the bitch off her feet. Oh my God, maybe she'll get laid and my problems will go away. This could be the answer to my prayers.

I run for the elevator as the clock clicks to 6:58.

*   *

I leave the elevator, head through the security turnstile, and head out the front door.

No one's waiting. No Rachel. No one who could be

Ramon. Just the lingering smell of hundreds of cigarettes. The front entrance is prime smoking territory. Another excuse folks use to take a break and waste time.

Rachel comes through the revolving door a minute later and gives me a big smile.

"Sorry I was off the grid today. I was stuck in meetings getting my designs beat to crap."

"Must be hard to put your heart into ideas that you think suck."

"You have no idea. Hey, Ramon!"

She leaps away from me and into the arms of a perfectly put together human being of the male species.

Ramon is six two, as mentioned by Rachel before, and he is muscular without being overly ripped. He is dressed so well but so cool that even the fashion peon that I am can recognize true greatness. He could be Hispanic, he could be African American, he could even be part Asian.

He lifts Rachel off the ground effortlessly and spins her around.

"Hey, girl."

He puts her down, and they both stare at me.

"Ramon, meet Ryan Simmons, my work BFF."

Ramon smiles, displaying big, white teeth, and looks me up and down. We shake hands, or rather we do the latest version of a shake with a bump and a new twist that I just try to go with so I don't seem like a total loser.

Then he takes a real look at me.

"Oh, lord, have mercy."

Rachel laughs.

"Yes, this is the project that I mentioned."

"You owe me big-time for this one, Rach."

"I know, I know. Look, I gotta get back inside. Have fun, you two."

She is gone before I can get a word in.

"Uh, nice to meet you, Ramon, but I have no idea what this is about."

Ramon puts his arm around my shoulders like an older brother about to impart sage advice.

"This, my new friend, is about the first day of your new life."

He looks down at my shoes.

"Are those Hush Puppies for real?"

*   *

Before I know it, we're in a cab heading downtown.

"I hope you didn't have any plans tonight, 'cause you're going to be out late. Real late."

"If you count watching *American Idol* as plans, then I had plans."

"Don't worry about that. We'll get updates on my iPhone."

"So, uh, where are we heading, my brother?"

Ramon gives me a look and wags his finger at me.

"'So, uh,' no! Do not refer to me as your brother like we're in some lame 1970s buddy movie."

"My bad."

"Oh man. This is gonna be harder than I thought. 'My bad' is so ancient it's got hair on it. How about you pretend you're a deaf-mute and just listen and let me do the talking?"

"If I'm deaf, then I won't be able to hear you."

"Now that was a good one. Maybe there is hope for you, white boy."

"How do you know Rachel?"

"Me and Rach go back to Parsons. Met the first day at orientation. If it wasn't for her, I probably never would have graduated. Too much bullshit for me, but she insisted I stick it out and get my ticket punched. I owe her for that."

The cab stops on Twenty-seventh Street between Sixth

and Seventh avenues. Ramon pays the driver, and we head off down the block.

"So here's the deal. Rach told me about your work situation, and that the two of you have to do the superhero thing and save the day. She also told me that you don't know jack about the world of high fashion." He eyeballs me from head to foot again. "And now that I've had the pleasure of meeting you, I believe her."

"What do you do now?"

"I'm somewhat of what you might call a unique individual. I have a very special job description. I'm a bit of a troubleshooter, a bit of a producer, a bit of a casting agent, a whole lot of a partier. All the big names use my services. I'm a fixer on the underside of the NYC fashion scene. You need a certain model for a certain shoot, but her agent says no, you call me. You need to borrow a few high-end outfits for your shoot, you call me. You got a photographer that's acting like a prima donna, you call me. You got your nerd-ball client in town and need to get into the hottest club, you call me.

"I don't do drugs, I don't do hookers, I don't do guns. Don't have to. Shit, the deputy mayor calls me when his daughters need new outfits.

"So here's the deal. You and me are gonna spend a few nights together. By the time we're done, you'll understand why good ol' House of Leary is going down the tubes. But first, we got to get you some new duds. I am not going to ruin my reputation by being seen with you dressed like that."

We enter a nondescript building through the freight entrance. The elevator opens, and Ramon exchanges greetings with the operator. We get off on the tenth floor, a huge open space filled with nothing but clothing racks. Ramon turns to me.

"Let's give the mute thing a try. You let me do the talking."

A gorgeous blonde squeals and then runs over and gives

Ramon a hug. I can't hear what they're saying, but after a few more hugs and a few kisses, Ramon signals to me and we hit the racks.

"This is the latest and the greatest. This is next fall's collection. This stuff hasn't even hit the stores yet."

He eyes me again.

"I'd say you're a 32 waist, 36 inseam, 16 1/2 neck, 35 sleeve, about a size 11 shoe. Sound about right?"

"Dead on."

We spend the next hour wandering around the showroom with me trying things on. I learn more in that hour than I ever thought possible. The different kinds of cotton. Thick belts versus thin. The different cuts of a jacket. Pleats versus no pleats. When to wear a narrow shoe, when to wear more pointed. Thick ties, thin ties, striped ties, patterned ties. The difference between leather that feels like a cow and leather that feels like cashmere.

"What did you tell blondie, by the way?"

"The usual. That you're a model I need to outfit for a shoot tomorrow for a vodka brand. You'll probably have to return everything, but we'll see."

"You da man."

"Mute."

"Mute. Got it."

We end up in the makeshift dressing room. I'm standing on a tailor's block looking at myself in those wraparound mirrors, and I must say the transformation is astounding. I mean, I look good. And I feel good. I could get used to this. I must be wearing several thousand dollars worth of threads.

"Don't get used to it, my fashion challenged friend, unless you got a rich uncle about to die."

But it's already too late. I'll never wear wash-and-wear again.

I'm looking at myself in the mirror, and something isn't

right. Ramon is already a step ahead of me. His iPhone is already at his ear.

"Hello, baby. How you doing? I'm fine, good. Just fine. You know me. But yes, I do have a bit of a situation. I got a boy here that's in a shoot tomorrow, and he needs you bad. Real bad. You can? Oh my God, you are a lifesaver. We'll be there in twenty."

We leave my old clothes in the garbage, Hush Puppies and all. I don't even look back.

*   *

We're back in a cab heading east. Fifteen minutes later we're in the East Village, walking down a flight of stairs to a basement entrance with no sign. Ramon knocks and the door opens a few seconds later.

We step in, and Ramon is immediately engulfed in a huge hug that jams his face right into perhaps the largest set of breasts in all of Manhattan.

"Ramon!"

"Hey, doll."

'Doll' is actually Sandra, a massive black woman about fifty years old who is just about the sexiest thing I've ever seen. She moves like a cat, and her perfume is to die for. I look around and see that I'm in a high-tech salon with walls covered with more photographs of celebrities than the mayor's office.

I stay mute.

"Sandra, this is Alexi. He's from Bulgaria or some shit, and he doesn't speak English. I need him for a vodka shoot tomorrow."

"What, they don't have hairdressers in Bulgaria?"

Sandra motions for me to take off my jacket and shirt, which she hangs up with care. She knows quality when she sees it. She motions for me to sit, and I lean back and let her wash my hair.

Getting my hair washed by Sandra is better than all of the sex I've had up to this point in my life. I feel myself drifting off as her huge fingers massage my scalp with a luxurious shampoo and then a conditioner that smells just like heaven itself.

When I come back to earth, I'm sitting in her chair staring at myself in the mirror as the two of them discuss my new do. I figure I'm in good hands.

Sandra attacks my locks with a focused energy that seems to send her into a trancelike state. Ramon sits and reads a magazine, occasionally glancing up and smiling. Even he doesn't dare interrupt Sandra as she works.

She finishes by putting a bit of product in my hair and doing a final shaping with her fingers.

Again, I'm ruined. I can no longer get my hair cut at the barber for $15. It's $65 plus tip at the salon for me. I'm going to become one of those people who look great as they file for personal bankruptcy.

I put my shirt and jacket back on and can't help but admire myself.

Even Ramon smiles.

"Damn."

Ramon pushes me toward the door, and I take the hint. He hugs and kisses Sandra, and I hear them speaking softly. He doesn't pay her, but the exchange is acknowledged within their own complicated system of barter: a favor for a favor either already given or to be given in the future.

I head back up to the sidewalk, and Ramon joins me there.

"So here I am, all dressed up and no place to go."

I've said it with an eastern European accent. Ramon smiles.

"Oh, we got places to go, Alexi, we got places to go."

*   *

We're back in a cab heading west. It's only ten o'clock, early for the NYC night scene, but things are starting to pick up. We stop outside the entrance to a club—MPD, for Meat Packing District—the hottest one currently in the city. There's a throng of Staten Island and New Jersey wannabees waiting behind the silk rope and two enormous Asian bouncers who look like sumo wrestlers who've been stuffed into black suits. They wear what seem to be permanent scowls on their faces.

We get out of the cab and walk straight up to the rope. I'm wrong. The bouncers break into wide smiles as soon as they see Ramon. The closer one grabs him in a bear hug and practically tosses him to his partner, who fake lunges at Ramon sumo style. They all laugh, and Ramon gestures at me to follow. Sumo dude #2 opens the door, and we waltz inside. The throng starts complaining loudly but is quickly silenced by scowls from the bouncers.

I'm beside myself. Once we're inside the door, I start dancing around.

"That was so cool!"

Ramon glares at me and sticks a finger in my face.

"Be cool, fool. It's all about attitude. You act like you don't belong here and it'll come true—you won't belong. Stick to the Alexi shit and say as little as possible. Let the chicks be intrigued. You're wearing $5,000 worth of clothing, and you've got a $500 haircut. Own that shit. Believe me, the babes will notice. Now just keep your mouth shut and follow my lead."

I haven't hit the club scene much, primarily because I can't afford it, I work too hard, and I probably wouldn't get much past the losers out front. But I could get into this.

The place is decorated like a slaughterhouse, with conveyor belts and huge meat hooks. Maybe it's not decorated. Maybe it was a slaughterhouse. Who knows?

The music is hypnotic, and the huge dance floor is filled

with writhing bodies, one more amazing than the next. I don't see an ugly person anywhere. Even the bartenders and cocktail waitresses must be models.

Ramon threads his way across the room, stopping every few feet to hug, kiss, or shake hands with a never-ending stream of people he knows. I start to become Alexi, trying to own my accent and attitude. I say little and jump in with an air kiss or hug when it seems appropriate.

"Remember, you're here to learn. Have fun but pay attention. I want you to notice what people are wearing. Look at their outfits, their jewelry, their shoes, and their accessories. Especially their accessories. That's where outfits are made or destroyed. And keep your ears open. I'm going to steer the conversation toward what's hot and what's not. What designers are in, who's coming down the pike, who's toast. Listen and learn, my friend. You are at the heart of where fashion happens."

We reach a seated area off to the side, guarded by another bouncer, who opens the rope and silently leads us to a table filled with eight of the most gorgeous examples of womanhood I've ever seen outside of a magazine. These are goddesses. These are the models that grace the covers of the most glamorous as well as the most slutty of magazines. These are Aphrodite returned to earth. They jump up with delight at the sight of Ramon and make room for us on the semicircular couch. I'm welcomed like an old friend and just go along with it.

The table in front of us resembles a butcher block, and it's filled with what's known as bottle service. These chicks don't order by the drink. They make their own cocktails from an array of expensive vodkas and mixers right at the table. Grey Goose, Absolut, Stoli—probably paid for by their agents and managers and those trying to get into their panties. We're talking easily over $100 a bottle.

Before I know it, I'm happily sandwiched between a leggy redhead and a buxom brunette, doing shots of Stoli. Ramon warns me with his eyes to slow down. The night is young, so I obey and start sipping instead.

The conversation flows as easily as the vodka. Ramon is extraordinarily deft at leading the conversation for my benefit. I've established with halting English, with Ramon filling in the blanks, that I'm in town for a shoot for a new Bulgarian vodka that's hitting the United States with a huge marketing budget. I'm the cover guy. They all coo and fawn over me when he tells them that they're still looking for my female comodel. It's truly beautiful to watch as the bullshit flows from him like a fine wine.

Once my creds have been established, he throws out topics that have my radar turned up high. The conversation covers pocketbooks, Chihuahuas, iPods, belts, shoes, shoes, and of course shoes, photographers, every top fashion house, Brangelina, perfumes, Twitter, lingerie, watches, the Grammy Awards, tattoos, Facebook, and bracelets. And then, the moment I've been waiting for. Ramon nonchalantly throws down the gauntlet.

"I hear Leary's got a kickin' new collection coming out next fall."

The table goes silent. I hold my breath. The goddesses look at each other for five long seconds. Then, as one, they burst out laughing.

It's worse than I thought.

*   *

Pitch Minus 8 Days—Wednesday

I'm sitting at my desk. It's eight thirty the next morning. I'm on my second cup of crappy black coffee from Momar on the corner. My head hurts, and I'm still in my clothes from last night. I never went home. We ended up at Coffee Shop on Union Square for breakfast at around five. My new pals went home to sleep until noon, while I went to work.

I pop a few more aspirin.

My IM blinks. It's the bitch. Oh shit.

Morning, Ry.

Hey.

Please, God, please, God, please, God, let it be that Don came through for us.

Soooooo?

He wants to get together! Can you believe it? He wants to get together!

Thank you, God.

That's fantastic. I told you to relax.

You were right. I'll trust you next time.

Am I hearing this correctly?

Ry, do you have those retouches yet?

Uhhhh, I'll have to check.

That's okay. Don't worry about it. Tomorrow's fine.

Tomorrow's fine? Don, whoever you are, you are now officially my best bud forever.

Great. I'll touch base later.

B.

I have to go rip Chas a new one for messing up with the retouches. But of course he won't be in until 10:00.

I look up into Rachel's smiling face.

"You look like shit. I mean, your clothes look great, but you look like crap."

"Thanks."

"So what do you think of Ramon?"

"Ramon is a god."

"Yes, he is amazing. So, what'd you learn?"

"That it's much worse than I thought."

"Leary?"

"Leary. It's off the grid. It's a hundred-year-old brand that's got amazing equity, but it's completely losing the next several generations."

"And our wonderful campaign will only hasten its demise."

"We're dead. The whole agency will be on the street. And my head hurts."

"Well, you better get some rest somehow. Ramon has another night planned for you. He won't tell me what he's got in store for you."

"Seven o'clock?"

"No, four. You'll have to duck out early. He said to wear jeans and a black T-shirt."

"Jeans and a black T-shirt. Check."

*   *

With the bitch out of my hair for a day, I spend the morning catching up. I run out at lunchtime to The Gap and buy jeans and a black T-shirt. I leave my new outfit at the dry cleaners around the corner.

I get back to my desk with a cheeseburger deluxe. I'm wolfing it down when my phone rings. It's Angie, Chas's boss. If it's possible, she's even more of a prima donna than Chas. I decide to pick up, even though I've got a huge bite in my mouth.

"Hey, Ange."

"Where are you? We're all waiting in the conference room."

"What are you talking about?"

I look at my Outlook and see that someone has snuck a

meeting onto my calendar. It wasn't there when I left an hour ago. "Flake-Off Creative Review—1:00 PM to 2:00 PM."

Chas.

"How about a little notice next time?"

"Chas tells me he told you about it yesterday."

"Chas is full of shit."

"I beg your pardon? Do you realize that you're on speakerphone with the whole creative team on your account?"

"I said, Chas is full of shit! Did everyone hear me, or do I have to repeat myself again?"

"You better watch it, Ry. I will not have you speak to any member of my team like that."

"I'll be there in a minute. And I'm bringing my burger. Is there any extra ketchup up there?"

This should be fun. High noon at the dandruff corral.

*   *

I grab my burger, fries, and Diet Coke and head up to the eleventh floor. I get off the elevator and head right toward the creative conference room, chewing as I go. I'm pissed. I'm tired. My head hurts. And I'm probably still a bit drunk. I'm ready for a fight.

I open the door and give the team a big smile. I sit down right next to Ange and take a big bite.

"Hi, everyone. Sorry I'm late."

It comes out fairly unintelligible between the burger, cheese, pickles, lettuce, and tomato, with three large fries stuffed in between "everyone" and "sorry" for emphasis.

I look around the table and make eye contact with everyone one at a time.

There's Henry the copywriter, who is writing a book and a screenplay and a blog and is under the illusion that this is just a temporary stopover on his way to fame and fortune. I've read his stuff. This isn't a temporary stop.

Then comes Marissa, the graphic designer superwoman. She can only be described as cool, calm, and collected. She's attractive in her own down-to-earth kinda way. She's the type to get things done without the usual creative posturing and hissy fits. She turns out more work in a day than most turn out in a week. She's saved my ass more times than I can count. And she's a genius when it comes to computers.

Then there's Chas, dressed in black. Glaring at me. And my burger.

I begin.

"So where are my retouched photos? They're late."

Figure I'll start by taking the offensive.

Ange counters.

"They're late because the photographer didn't release the files to us until she knew she'd get paid."

Oh, nice one.

"That's rich. When was the last time you let a photographer get away with that? We pay most of our vendors like sixty days after we get their invoice. If they're lucky and if the client has paid us. Don't give me that BS."

Chas decides to pipe up.

"That's not true. We never demand original files until we've paid. That's standard."

"Not in this lifetime. Maybe back in the days when the photographer you selected last had a job."

"She did a great job."

"You're right. She did. She did such a great job that we have to spend an extra $3,500 on retouching."

"We have a retouching budget. We always do."

"You're right—$750 for an hour of work, not $3,500 for zit removal."

Ange breaks in.

"Zit removal?"

Marissa is looking down and trying not to crack up.

"Yes, zit removal. Why don't you ask Chas about it."

"So the talent had some bad skin. It happens."

I've finished my burger. I stand.

"Why are we here? This is bull. The bitch is already bitching about getting the shots. Let me know when you have them, so I can get her off my back."

I leave. Man that felt good. I've never been such a dick before. That was fun.

I get dirty looks as I cross the floor to the elevators.

*   *

I spend the afternoon redoing some budgets. What fun. The good news is that I figured out a way to cover the extra $2,750 in retouching. I had $3,000 in for online banners, which I can pretend was supposed to be in the interactive budget. Let them eat it. They can bury it somewhere in the dandruff game.

I feel good about my cleverness with numbers when my phone Tweets.

Good news! Dad agreed to Silvia Weinstock for the cake. Sweet Sweet Sweet!!!

Gag.

*   *

As it nears four o'clock, I'm itching to start my next adventure. I'm pacing out front when Ramon waves from a cab window and motions for me to hop in. I do and we're off.

"How ya feeling?"

"Okay, I guess. I'm running on adrenaline at this point. You look fresh."

"Seven hours of sleep."

"You suck."

Ramon laughs. We head north and then east. I have no clue where we're heading until the cab pulls over on Sixty-sixth Street just east of Park Avenue. The Armory. I've seen it but never been inside.

The Armory is the height of culture. It puts on shows ranging from ancient art to contemporary auctions. I've never been inside. I've never been invited. I'm not cool enough or rich enough or famous enough to be on their mailing list.

We get out of the cab and head toward the back of the building, where there's a back entrance that is bustling with activity. We approach the loading docks, which are heavy with security. Everyone wears a security badge around their necks. We, of course, don't have security badges.

I wonder what will happen as we approach the entrance. Silly me. The security guy, a huge Rasta type with dreadlocks to his ass, hugs Ramon like a long-lost brother.

"Can you buzz Dougie for me?"

"You got it."

Rasta clicks his high-tech walkie-talkie/mike thing as we head in without any further ado.

*   *

The first thing I notice is that everyone on the crew is wearing jeans and a black T-shirt. This is my first clue.

We enter the main room of the Armory to a scene of pure and utter chaos. We're approaching what must be a stage from the back. Thick wires and cables crisscross the floor. A makeshift control area sits against the back wall, where several technicians play on high-end MacBook Pros. Lights flash as they do their testing. Music blares on and off as another set of audio techs adjust their levels.

From a side door emerges the biggest, baddest, gayest goateed individual I have ever seen. Despite his massive size, he moves with a grace that belies his bulk. He's geared up with a headset, a walkie-talkie, and a cell phone, and he appears to be speaking into all three at the same time.

He, too, is wearing a black T-shirt and jeans. Jeans that could probably fit three or four of me.

"Ramon!"

"Dougie!"

What follows is a twenty-second routine of hugs, knuckle punches, hip bumps, and 1980s dance moves that has to be seen to be believed. It ends with a huge hug and an even huger belly laugh.

"Ramon, it's been too long."

"Dougie, my man."

They both stop and stare at me with their arms crossed.

I feel like a New York strip steak as Dougie eyes me up and down. I stand still as he takes a slow walk around me.

"Okay, he'll do."

Ramon gives Dougie another hug and points his finger at me. "You behave yourself. And do everything that Dougie here tells you to do."

Ramon is gone before I can even muster a question. Dougie puts a huge paw on my shoulder and begins a monologue that I'm smart enough to just shut up and listen to.

"This is a private show for Leary's fall collection. And when I say private, I mean private. This is the hottest ticket in town, and you're going to see everything. You're also going to work your cute little ass off."

"Rule number one—you're gay. You'll understand why soon enough, and you'll thank me for it. Trust me. So let's see it, girlfriend."

I look at him blankly.

"Uhhhh—"

"C'mon, Ryan. Let's see you strut. Let's see your inner gay man striving to be free."

He skips around waving his arms. I try to imitate him. I fail.

"Ryan, Ryan, Ryan. Now that was pathetic. That was from the outside in. You need to be gay from the inside out. Now strut."

He takes off at a fast walk around to the front of the stage. I try to keep up with him. I try to swing my hips. I loosen my arms and let them swing.

The front of the stage is a gorgeous runway. As chaotic as it is in back, the front is a true work of art. It's everything that one would expect from having seen fashion runways on television. Dougie walks right up on stage and begins a runway strut to end all runway struts.

I realize in horror that I'm supposed to follow him. I do, but I'm still straight. I'm not gay yet. Even worse, more and more members of the crew have started wandering out front to watch. As the audience grows, Dougie plays to the crowd like a true pro.

"Marcel—lights! I need lights! I need you to make me beautiful!"

The house lights immediately go down, and several spots of various hues hit Dougie.

"Lawrence—music! I need music! I need to move, Lawrence. I need a beat, Lawrence. Give me a beat!"

The entire room explodes with sound. The crowd of gay boys starts to move as one. Dougie struts the runway as they all call out to him. He varies between working a serious model strut and blowing air kisses to the adoring crowd.

I gulp as he turns to me. I take a deep breath and plunge in. I prance around the stage. I try to feel the music. I try to let go.

Dougie claps his hands twice. The music stops immediately.

"I'm going to write a screenplay. I'm going to call it

Straight Men Can't Dance, and you're going to be the star. Back to work, ladies!"

He takes my arm and leads me backstage.

"We'll try it this way. Forget about the inner gay. Just pretend. Just act and speak however you think a gay guy would act. Talk with a lisp and wave your arms a lot."

We approach a thin wisp of a man who must be Dougie's #2.

"Raul, this is Ryan. Ryan, Raul. Raul runs everything while I just look good and get paid the big bucks. This is the big time, Ryan, and you've got a backstage pass. If you keep your eyes and ears open, you'll learn more tonight than you'd learn in three years at FIT."

The next hour is a total blur. Raul has me running around like a general gopher, doing everything from helping to run cable, to adjusting lights, to setting up racks and racks of outfits and accessories.

I start to put things together as I watch things coming together. The dressing areas backstage are prepped for each model. Each model will have to make five to ten outfit changes as the evening progresses. There's no time for mistakes. Timing is key.

As time passes, more and more people start to arrive. Joining the crew are the hairstylists and makeup artists. They all seem to know where to set up, with numbers guiding them to their stations.

The buzz in the place gradually picks up, and by six thirty the entire backstage area is invisible to the front. I spend the next half hour helping set up three bars near the entranceway.

I'm then sent back into the dressing areas, and my life changes forever. The real girls have arrived. Raul pulls me aside.

"I want you to spend the next forty-five minutes helping out the girls. They're going to need everything under the sun—lipstick, pads, tape, water, Tampax, and God knows what else. You're one of five floaters who are just there to get them what they need. Some will treat you like shit, and some will be as sweet as can be. Just ignore their personalities and get them what they need. The show must go on."

He pushes me into the dressing area, and now I understand why Dougie said I'd thank him. And why I have to be gay.

Eight of the top models in the world are in various states of undress right in front of me. Boobies to the left of me, ass cheeks to the right. I'll do anything to stay here. My wrists go limp and my hips soften. I never knew I had such a pronounced lisp.

"Hey, you there, help me tape this on."

A stunning brunette with the most perfect breasts I have ever seen is holding her outfit and pointing toward a roll of special double-sided tape. I pretend to know exactly what I'm doing as she practically puts her right nipple in my mouth while I attach the tape over her left boob. She places the right part of the outfit over the tape, and I very graciously help her pat it into place.

"Make sure it's on tight."

I pat a few more times, just to be sure.

"Gorgeous." I lisp. "Just gorgeous."

If I could slow down time, this would be the time to do it. Unfortunately, the next forty-five minutes pass all too quickly. I never knew being a slave could be so much fun.

But, true to my mission, I'm soaking it all in. I'm listening to the banter between the hair and makeup folks. I'm watching the dynamics of the underlying pecking order of which models are with which labels. I'm watching the designers themselves as they check in and make final adjustments to outfits and accessories. The air is tense and exciting, and you can almost taste the buzz.

It's 7:25, and the models are all set for their first walks. Dougie finds me and leads me to his special hawk's perch, where he can see everything, from the front of the house to backstage.

"I owe you one, my GFF."

"GFF?"

"Gay friend forever."

He laughs. And the education of Little Tree continues.

"Look out front where the crowd is having drinks. Starting on the left and working our way around, there are the top four people from Leary. The blonde is Annette. Just Annette. She's the real power behind the throne. She's Mitchell's first daughter, and she's been running the place for the last five years. She's as cold as ice and all business. She controls more advertising dollars than anyone in the industry, and she knows it. I don't have to tell you that. She's the one who kicked the old agency to the street and probably enjoyed doing it. Next to her is Mitchell Leary, the godfather himself. Still the most powerful man in fashion despite their lagging sales and Annette's power plays. Then there's Maurice Silvestre. He's married to Leary's other daughter, who stays out of the business altogether. Their marriage is good, amazingly enough. And then there's Katrina, better known as the Viper. She's the head of product development, and she's as nasty as they come. She knows that her days are numbered if things don't turn around in the next year or so, and she's only getting nastier. The rest of the first row is their entourage of assistants, ass kissers, fawners, and design staff.

"Over there are the editors and publishers and designers from all of the top glamour books. There's *Vogue*, *Glamour*, *Cosmopolitan*, and all the others. These are the men and woman who make or break careers in the same room as the one group of people that they kowtow to—the fashion advertisers who fill their ad pages. These are people who don't make nice to anyone, making nice to people they usually hate with a passion.

"Over there, drinking like fish, are various agents,

managers, and other hangers-on and ass kissers. There are also celebrities who like to see and be seen as well as assorted other members of the rich and famous.

"The show will go for about forty-five minutes. Everyone here has ADD, so that's about all they can stand, sitting in one place. Right now, go out front and help Paul at the middle bar. He'll be glad for the help. This is where the real action happens. Watch the interactions and listen to the conversations. This is prime time to learn what people really think. Take a tray and walk around and pick up empties, or walk around and hand out drinks. And listen, listen, listen.

"Once everyone heads in for the show, I want you to watch out front. You see Raul over there on the side—go hang with him and help him out if he needs it.

"Once the show is over, head back into the dressing area and help out again. I know, I know, you can thank me later. This is also prime time. The girls get a vibe as they walk the runway. Listen to their comments as they come in and change. They hate it when their outfits make them look bad—it's more competitive among them than you could ever imagine. They're all huggy huggy, but they'd slice each other to ribbons if they thought they could get away with it."

I give him a hug. It's all I can think to say.

"Go, go. Get out of here. I've got work to do, young grasshopper."

*   *

Paul smiles as I approach and is all business.

"We've got a red, a white, Pellegrino, and Diet Coke. The red is a '94 Clos du Bois cab. The white is a Sonoma '02 sauvignon blanc. Believe me, they'll ask."

"And the Diet Coke, '08 or '09?"

He smiles.

"Wiseass."

Within seconds I'm working like a dog. It's very interesting to see how "the help" is treated. Some look through us, as if we're not even there. Others couldn't be nicer, with smiles and pleases and thank-yous. And it isn't related to the food chain—it's the people themselves.

After the initial onslaught, I fill up a tray with half reds and half whites and start wandering the room. I roam from group to group and listen intently.

From what I'm hearing, it might not be such a good night for Leary.

My tray is almost empty when I look up and see something that makes my heart stop cold. Across the room is none other than Drew himself. Duh. Of course he'd be here. Of course he'd be invited.

He's standing with the gang from Leary and—Holy shit, I don't believe it!—the head creatives from the other three agencies in the review. All making nicey nice. It's one of the funniest things I've ever seen. Fake smiles and small talk and "Aren't we all the best of friends, but I'd murder your children if it meant we'd win the account."

I should know better, but I go back to Paul and fill up my tray. I'm thinking how unlikely it is that Drew will recognize me. I've only been in one meeting with him, and there had to be at least twenty other people there. Let's face it, I'm a peon. He won't recognize me. Especially out of context. And if I'm gay with a new $500 haircut.

I decide I can't resist. I keep my eyes focused on the ground, and I head over.

Annette is holding court. Drew and the other three, a guy and two women, are falling over themselves and hanging on her every word. She could say that she loves eating raw chicken sushi, and they'd agree that it's absolutely delicious.

Drew takes a red wine from my tray and glances at me funny for half a second, but then he turns quickly to laugh at what Annette just said. They're all trying extremely hard to talk about anything except the review while hoping for some tiny bit of insight at the same time.

I'm learning nothing new as I make my way around the group beyond that the women prefer white and the guys red. The woman from Porter Crisp seems the most nervous and out of her league, while the guy from B&K seems overly confident. He keeps touching Annette—probably a mistake. Mitchell is chatting with the woman from BDD, but he's paying more attention to her breasts than to what she's saying. All's fair. If she hasn't already slept with him, I'm sure she will soon.

Drew is wisely playing it cool, I have to give him credit for that.

Then the shocker: Annette decides to bring up business, and they all take heed. I'm working the group nearby by now, but I'm all ears.

"We're looking forward to all of your presentations. I hope you've all taken it to heart that we're really looking for something new. I can already tell we're going to get trashed in our fall reviews by all of our dear friends here in the media. We can survive another lousy season. But that's it. We're willing to do whatever it takes to ensure that our legacy lasts for another hundred years. And we're counting on you, or should I say one of you, to help lead the way."

With that, Silvestre takes her arm, and the Leary team head toward their seats. The four agency people stare at each other awkwardly for a second and then head in different directions.

I bring my tray back to the bar, say later to Paul, and head to find Raul as the lights flash and the crowds head to their seats.

The show itself is pretty amazing. It's one thing to watch something like this on E! as a ten-second clip but quite another to see the whole thing live. I enjoy hanging with Raul and watching as he deftly makes tiny adjustments here and there via short, precise whispers into his headset. He knows his shit. I run a few errands for him throughout and then head backstage again when the lights come up.

*   *

I spend the next half hour in the dressing rooms with the "girls" and the girls. I find myself becoming more and more oblivious to the flesh surrounding me—maybe I truly am channeling my inner gay man.

The consensus among the eight models seems to be that Leary has clearly rounded out the bottom of all of the fall shows with stuff that looks too much like last year, which was the beginning of the downturn. The models have made it clear what contracts they want for next year, and what contracts they might be able to get out of.

The girl girls are gone by nine thirty, and the rest of Dougie's crew break everything down in astonishing speed. Everyone knows his role. I help out where I can, and everyone seems to appreciate my presence.

We're all wrapped by eleven thirty, and then it's time to party. Try as I might to sneak off and go home, I'm dragged with the gang down to a hot spot in the West Village, were we take over the dance floor and commandeer the bar. Before I know what's happened, I'm dancing in a conga line of sorts with my hands in the air and Raul behind me and Paul in front of me.

Who says I'm not open to new experiences? Two gay guys already have my phone number. Who knows?

Around four in the morning, I'm finally able to sneak away and head home. I spend $40 on a cab, as I don't think I'd even make the three-block walk to the subway.

*   *

Pitch Minus 7 Days—Thursday

I'm back at my desk at eight thirty the next morning. My head hurts.

Annette was certainly right about the reviews. Everything I'm reading online says things like "uninspired" and "so last year." To a fashion house, words like these are death.

Even more interesting, apparently *Advertising Weekly* was at the show last night, and there's a picture of Annette and the gang of four—and yes, believe it or not, the back of my head. I thank every god I've ever heard of that my face is not in the picture.

To say the interest in the review has been intense is to put it mildly. A huge account, the glitter of the fashion world, outsized personalities—it's all too good to be true for the industry rags.

The article is the second in a series. The first, which ran several weeks ago, covered the announcement of the review itself with the associated bland quotes from the client and the incumbent agency. This came out before it was known which agencies were included in the review. The article today, titled "The Final Four," is a rather in-depth piece on each of the four agencies, with a special focus on the head creatives.

In keeping with industry tradition, no one from any of the agencies has discussed the review with the press. This would be bad form and bad luck. But this doesn't prevent the writer, Janice Stone, from doing her own history of the four.

The part about H&V harkens back to the better days when the agency was a creative powerhouse. It almost waxes poetic about Peter Vine. It basically concludes that the work since Drew took over has been adequate, but that "the jury is still out" on whether or not he'll make a true mark on the industry. This is his "big test."

And no article about H&V would be complete without the asking of the question that no one seems to know the answer to—Where is Peter Vine? It's the great mystery of the advertising world.

Perhaps it's time to tell what did happen with Vine, at least as much as I know. I'm not sure how accurate it is, but I've heard it enough times that it must at least be close to the truth.

The legend goes that Vine and Halliday were having dinner at the Four Seasons with the top-three people from Grocter & Pramble, their biggest client and the biggest advertiser in the world. The G&P people were exploring the possibility of consolidating several huge accounts with H&V: we already handled three major brands, and they were discussing having us handle up to four more. We're talking an increase from $150 million in billings to almost $400 million.

Things were going great and it looked like they had it in the bag when Vine starts losing it. He was on some very powerful drugs for depression, but he had stopped taking them a few days before. Bad timing. Really bad timing. Halliday sees what's happening—he's seen it before—but it's too late for him to really do anything to stop it. And it gets bad.

Vine starts telling the G&P people that he thinks that many of their brands have become too powerful and that it's not really good for the country. He goes off on this wild explanation about connections between advertising and television and brands and that they have too much control. The G&P people don't really know how to respond. And then it gets worse. Vine goes off on mind control and the television networks. Finally Halliday has to get the manager to call an ambulance, and Vine ends up in the emergency room under sedation.

Needless to say, G&P didn't consolidate their brands at H&V. Over the next several months, they put the three existing accounts into review. Also needless to say is that The Duke did not take well to losing $150 million in billings, not to mention the $250 million left on the table. Before we knew it, Vine was gone and Drew showed up on our doorstep.

The story eventually came out, and *Advertising Weekly* and the others had a field day. It only made it better that Peter Vine disappeared. Rumors flew—that he was in a mental hospital, that he and his wife moved to Africa or Australia, that he committed suicide—it finally died down after a few months. But Vine is still missing.

Halliday never blamed Vine. He loved the guy, despite his problems. He defended him until the end, and I think he still misses him. I sure miss him, even though I only got to speak with him a few times.

So Drew is not going to like this article. He hates it when he is compared to Vine. I would too if I were him and I had no talent. I'm sure he's already in a bad mood, which is kind of a nice thought.

For me, I can tell it's going to be a bad day. My leaving early yesterday was obviously not a good move. Meetings have been put onto my calendar that I would have not accepted had I been here.

I have thirty-two e-mails and seven voice mails. My cell was off for most of the night, and it's got four text messages, three Tweets, and five messages.

I check my cell first. The first message is from Kristina, one of the models from MPD. I can't believe it. I vaguely remember making out with her in the unisex bathroom-lounge thing and seem to recall that it was rather pleasant.

"Hi, Alexi, it's Kristina. Hope you remember me from last night. Listen, I was calling to see if my agent could call you and see if you could hook me up for that vodka shoot. I'd really appreciate it! Bye!

Great. She's more interested in my fake ability to hook her up than getting me into bed. Rats.

Two of the other messages are from the bitch, just saying

"Call me." And the other two are from Rach, checking in to see how I'm doing.

The Tweets are both from my ex.

Invites so gorgeous. Classy. Classy. Classy.
Menu to die for. Die for. Die for!!!

One of the texts is also from Kristina. Same deal. Two others are from Ramon—checking in late last night. Must have been while I was on the conga line. The last came in this morning from Paul, asking where I disappeared to last night and wondering if I'd like to have a drink sometime.

Perfect. Now I have two people after me—a model who thinks I'm Bulgarian and can cast her in a major print shoot, and a gay guy who thinks I'm also gay.

I reply to Ramon.

"I've decided I'm gay. Thanks for helping me out of the closet."

I call the bitch, thinking she won't be in yet. Wrong.

"It's about time you got back to me, Ry. What the hell is going on with you? And where the hell are my retouches?"

Don is a dead man. Wherever he is, he's dead. Chas, too. Chas is dead.

"Well, good morning to you, Rebecca."

"I'm not in the mood, Ry. I want your ass over here in thirty minutes, with the retouches."

Slam. You know, in a way, I think I like her better this way. I dial Marissa.

"Hey, Ry."

"Please tell me you have the retouches. I need them. Now."

"Ahhhhh—"

"Talk to me."

"Chas decided that the shots weren't good enough. Didn't meet our standards. Ange agreed. He set up another shoot for tomorrow."

"You're kidding me. Please tell me you're kidding me."

"I'm kidding you. But I'm not. And I haven't told you the best part. He's using his girlfriend again."

"Goddamn it! Is he in yet?"

"No, he called in sick."

"Do you still have the files?"

"Of course."

"I'll be right up. Don't move. Bring up the files."

"You got it."

I grab my cell and run to the elevator.

＊　　　＊

Marissa is waiting for me with the files open.

"You've been working on these, haven't you?"

"Yeah, our usual guy did the heavy lifting, but I stayed last night and did some more work."

"They look great."

"Chas said they suck. Said the bitch would never approve them."

"I've got to get over there. Can you fit them on a flash drive?"

"Consider it done."

She hands me the drive.

"Listen to me, Marissa. Do not let Chas know that you gave this to me. You don't even know about it. I hacked onto the creative drive and took them myself."

"Okay, Ryan. Appreciate it."

"I wasn't here!"

And I'm off.

＊　　　＊

I don't even go back to my desk. I head down the elevator and make my way downtown. I've got fifteen minutes to go ten blocks. Shouldn't be a problem.

I call Rach. She doesn't answer.

I pop my e-mail to my phone and scan through them quickly. The thirty-two have grown to forty-five. At least half are unimportant, and five are from the bitch, but nothing new.

Then I see one from Chas, with copies to Bruce and Ange, outlining why he "must in good conscious" schedule a second shoot for the dandruff shots. He blames everything on me because I disrupted the shoot. He's lays it out in agonizing detail, concluding that he has no choice but to redo everything. He indicates how important it is that we uphold our quality standards and that "it's one of those times that we'll just have to absorb the cost in order to do the right thing."

I then open Ange's response, which is 100 percent supportive and suggests that "disruptive account personnel" should not be allowed on shoots in the future. She has taken the liberty to copy Drew on the thread.

Bruce's response, to me only, is quite simple. "Come explain this to me immediately."

I decide I better check my voice mail—three older ones from the bitch asking about the retouches, and two from Bruce asking where I am and telling me I better get my ass into his office to explain myself.

Hmmmmm.

How to play it. Ignore them until I get back, hopefully with the bitch's approval? Stop and try to type a full response with my thumbs? Call Bruce and tell him what's going on? Find out where Chas lives, get a gun, and shoot him and his untalented girlfriend in the kneecaps? Hmmmmm.

And now the ante has been upped by Ange bringing Drew into it.

I could sic the trolls on Chas by e-mailing them with my concerns about nepotism.

This is getting interesting. I'm not sure what to do. But I do know that in the words of Bugs Bunny, "Dis means war."

*   *

I make my way through the lobby of American Brands—I have my own spiffy vendor pass—and head up to the twelfth-floor conference room.

When I get off the elevator, my phone rings. It's Bruce. I click Ignore and put the phone on vibrate. Nothing pisses off the bitch more than when my phone keeps ringing in meetings.

As expected, she's waiting for me, looking at her watch even though I'm not late. She's surrounded by her two brand assistants, who I refer to as Mary-Kate and Ashley. They're living proof that it is possible to be too thin. I'm not sure if either one of them can speak. They both just kind of give me dirty looks and nod their heads in agreement when the bitch speaks.

I say hello and take my usual seat. The bitch wastes no time in lashing into me. I let her vent about how late the retouches are, how unacceptable this is, how this always happens, how it better not be over budget, and how this is holding up ten other things.

She assumes I don't have anything, as I've arrived seemingly empty-handed. I take the flash drive out of my pocket and hold it up.

She almost seems disappointed.

I crawl under the table and insert the drive into the USB port on the computer housed there.

I turn on the projector and open up the shots.

I present the different shots like the account pro that I am. I've given her several different angles and lighting techniques to choose from. I've got the model, now with perfectly clear skin, in three different shirts.

I've learned to give her a few selections, to recommend the worst one so she can overrule me, and to focus her on false choices that I couldn't care less about. This way she can impress her assistants and make me look bad at the same time.

But as I knew she would, she makes her selects and approves the two I knew she'd like anyway.

I think for a minute and then ask her if she can e-mail me her approval of shots four and seven, and, if she wouldn't mind, to Cc Chas, Ange, and Bruce.

She rolls her eyes at such a difficult request but nods. "Can you come to my office for a sec? I need to discuss something with you."

Mary Kate and Ashley disappear back to their cubes without a word or smile. I follow the bitch down to her office. She indicates that I should close the door.

She sits at her desk and starts clicking and typing.

"There—approval is sent."

"Thanks."

Little does she know the shit storm she has just unleashed. She indicates that I should sit.

"I need your advice."

I sit.

"Don get wiggy on you?"

"How'd you guess?"

"You like this guy, don't you?"

"I think so. I mean, as much as you can like someone that you haven't even met."

"Good point. So what happened?"

"Well, we've been e-mailing and IMing for the past few days. Figuring out how to get together. Would I come to Philly, or would he come to New York? We decided that he'd come up here this Saturday."

"So far so good."

"That's what I thought. Then I get an e-mail from him saying he can't make it, and that he'll contact me next week."

"Did he say why?"

"Nope."

"No explanation?"

"Nada."

"Strange."

"C'mon, you're a guy, tell me what it means—just changing his mind like that and going incommunicado on me."

"Pretty normal."

"C'mon."

"You want me to be honest?"

"Honest."

"He's met a few women he likes online, and he's trying to manage it. He was trying to meet you as well as someone else this weekend, and the other plans firmed up before yours. He got wiggy because he's uncomfortable lying, so he dealt with it by going incommunicado."

"That's amazing."

"What?"

"You're probably right."

"Now you just need to decide whether you can handle his juggling around, or if you have to move on."

"We'll see."

I stand to leave. My phone is vibrating. I hit Ignore again.

"Better get back and get the gang going on the layouts."

"Bye."

"Bye."

*   *

My phone is vibrating. I turn the ringer back on. It's Bruce.

"Hey, Bruce."

"Where the hell have you been?"

"With my client."

"Showing unapproved art without a creative present?"

"Chas is out today. The retouches were already late, and the client demanded to see them."

"I've got Ange and now Drew all over my ass."

"The client loved them. She approved them. Check your e-mail."

"I saw the goddamn e-mail. That's beside the point."

"It's besides the point that the client approved them?"

"The retouches you took over were not signed off by creative. You know the rules, Ryan."

"Yes, I know the rules, Bruce.

"Just get your ass back here."

*   *

My phone rings again as soon as I hang up. I don't recognize the number but answer it anyway.

"Ryan."

"Hello, Ryan, it's Paul."

Oh no. It's my new gay pal. I decide to be straight with him. Hahahaha. That wasn't even on purpose.

"Hey, Paul. Listen, I think I should tell you that—"

"You're not gay?"

"Uhhhh, yeah."

"Listen, Ryan. You've heard of gaydar, right? Well it works the other way as well. All of us, except the real girls of course, knew you weren't gay."

"You knew?"

"Of course, silly. You were having much too much fun backstage."

""Well don't I feel stupid. I thought you were calling to ask me out."

"So why am I calling? Is that what you're wondering?"

"I guess."

"Well, Mr. Ryan, it's just possible that a bunch of us really liked you and thought you were fun, and we wanted to invite you to a small dinner party this Saturday. You're welcome to bring a girlfriend or just come by yourself."

"Wow, that's really nice. I'm guess I'm just a little surprised."

"Surprised that gay people have straight friends?"

"Wow! Now I feel even stupider."

"I'll text you the address and details when we get off. It will be fun, I guarantee it, and we'll continue your education about fashion. Trust me, no one knows more about fashion than the New York City gay man."

*   *

I finish my walk and head into our building. I guess I should be scared knowing what I'm about to walk into, but I'm not. I get Paul's text as I get off the elevator, and it makes me smile. He tells me not to wear tight pants and to bring a bottle of wine and a decadent dessert.

With friends like Paul, I can handle a few enemies.

I head straight to Bruce's office. He gets up and closes the door behind me. We both sit.

"I don't need this kind of shit, Ryan."

"Neither do I."

"You're going to have to tell your client that we're redoing the shots and she's going to have to cough up the budget."

"You're kidding, right?"

"I'm not kidding, Ryan."

"She already approved them. She thought they were fine."

"Well, Chas and Ange and Drew think they don't reflect well on our standards."

"So let me get this straight. Our own creative team is more important than the client?"

"I wouldn't put it that way."

"I'm all ears."

"We have rules, Ryan. We have standards. We're a team. We can't have account people running around making creative decisions."

"Whose side are you on, Bruce?"

"I'm on nobody's side, Ryan. I'm on the agency's side. We're a team."

"Well, maybe you should have this conversation with Chas. And Ange. And Drew for that matter."

"I need you to call the client right away and tell her we're reshooting tomorrow."

"I can't do that."

"What do you mean you can't do that?"

"Let me give you a little heads-up, Bruce. The reason the shots sucked so bad was that Chas used his girlfriend as the photographer. I told him not to, but he insisted and said she was the best. Then his girlfriend decided to use her brother as the model, and he had skin so bad that we had to spend an extra $2,750 in retouching—which I've managed to cover, by the way, partly by cutting the fee to Chas's incompetent girlfriend.

"So we did the retouching, and the shots were fine. The brother is actually good-looking once you get past the zits. So Chas is actually using this as a chance to get his girlfriend even more money, and I refuse."

"This is all your fault."

"What?"

"It's your fault for letting Chas use his girlfriend to begin with. You should have put your foot down, and you should have come to me if Chas didn't back down."

I'm stunned by his logic. He's not totally wrong. But I'm still stunned.

"Well, I guess I've got to correct that mistake now. I'm going to my desk, and I'm e-mailing the trolls that I have to report an agency policy violation of nepotism. Thanks for the advice, Bruce. And it's also nice to know you have my back when I need you."

I get up, open the door, and leave his office.

"Ryan! Get back here!"

I keep walking.

*   *

I do exactly what I said I was going to do. I boot up, open my Outlook, and address an e-mail to the troll in charge of finance and the troll in charge of compliance. I write:

> Gentlemen—
>
> I must bring a serious matter to your attention. I apologize for not mentioning this sooner, but I was trying to respect my creative team, and quite honestly, I didn't want to be a rat. But I was wrong and should have contacted both of you immediately.
>
> My creative director, Chas Burnett, insisted that I use his current girlfriend as a photographer on the shoot of May 5 for the Flake-Off brand. He is now also insisting that we reshoot, using the same girlfriend. The new shots are completely unnecessary, as the client just approved the first set of shots.
>
> I also wish to point out that the incompetence of the photographer caused an unnecessary budget risk of $2,750 for retouching, which I am confident I can cover from other budget lines. Redoing the entire shoot will create a budget risk of at least an additional $10,000.

Again, I apologize for not bringing
Chas Burnett's violation of company policy
to your attention earlier, but now that the
situation has escalated, with additional
budgetary risk, I feel that I have no choice
but to bring it to your attention.
I will be happy to provide additional
information about this matter upon request.

Ryan Simmons

I copy Bruce, Chas, and Ange. I hesitate for a minute.
Should I really do this? Then I make my decision and hit
Send.

*   *

I want to see Rachel before the shit hits the fan. Prior to
her getting on the pitch team, we had lunch almost every day.
I miss my friend.

I text her to see if she can have lunch and am surprised
when she texts right back that she can. I text back to meet me
at Ar in fifteen minutes.

*   *

Rachel and I always prefer to sit at the bar rather than
getting a table or booth. Today I want to just hide in a booth.
I really want to order a beer but figure I better have all my wits
together when I get back.

My poor cell phone is acting schizoid again. I turn the
sound off. I put it on the table and just watch it vibrate. It
starts to move toward the edge of the table and I think how
much simpler my life would be if I let it just fall off and crash
to the floor.

Rach walks in the door, gives me a huge smile, and joins me in the booth. We both start talking at the same time.

"I have so much to tell you!" we both say, and then I tell her to go first.

"The stuff is so bad, and it's just getting worse. I feel like it's a big joke, like, we're not really presenting this stuff, are we?"

Something clicks way off in the back of my brain when she refers to the work as a joke. I don't know what it means, so I just store it away.

"How does the rest of the team feel about it?"

"It's hard to tell. Most of them are so afraid of Drew that they just keep their mouths shut. The better ones like Lou and Julie have tried to make other suggestions, but Drew just cuts them off at the knees. And of course, Chas does his dirty work behind the scenes to keep everyone toeing the party line."

I tell her what I overheard at the show the other night.

"They are really looking for something different. How does Drew justify that his crap is different?"

"He says that all clients say they want something new and innovative and different, and that they really don't mean it. They'll only stray so far from their comfort zone."

"You know, he's not wrong. That's usually true. But I think they mean it. I think they want out of their comfort zone. Way out."

"Well, he's Drew and he knows best."

"So there's nothing new from what I saw a few days ago?"

"A bit but not really. I have a drive for you."

She slides it across the table.

"Be careful where you watch it."

I take the drive and put it in my pocket.

"Of course."

"So tell me what's going on with you."

Jimmy wanders over and takes our order.

I start by telling her about my first night with Ramon—the clothes, the haircut, the mysterious Alexi, the clubs, everything. Then I tell her all about my night with Dougie and the girls and the girls. I tell her everything—my attempt to be gay, Dougie and the runway, the wild dancing at the gay bar. Before we know it, we're both laughing our asses off.

"So you fooled the real girls but not the gay boys."

"Not even close. As Paul explained, gaydar works both ways. So can you join me on Saturday?"

"I wouldn't miss it for the world."

This makes me even happier than I thought it would.

"Great. So now for the bad news. I could be in a heap of trouble."

I tell her about the whole thing with Chas. I show her the e-mail I just sent to the trolls.

"So it's safe to assume that Bruce will throw you under the bus?"

"You know, I'm not sure. Now that I've involved the trolls, he might have to support me. We'll see. He is a survivor, if nothing else."

"I think it will be obvious that Chas is the real culprit. You could have reported the whole thing earlier, but he's the one who really broke the rules."

"I'm hoping that the trolls will be more concerned about wasting money than any of the other crap."

"Do you think the trolls are scared of Drew?"

"Good question. I'm really not sure."

"I guess we'll find out."

We eat in silence for a few minutes. Rachel finally asks the real question.

"So what are we going to do about the pitch?"

I play with the remainder of my fries.

"You should have seen Annette at the show. She's one tough lady. She will not buy into any bullshit. They have a multibillion-dollar business that's going down the tubes, and they don't know what to do about it. This isn't just about a new ad campaign. This is about staying relevant. Things are changing so fast, and they have no clue how to deal with it."

"Drew doesn't get that at all."

"But to answer your question, I don't know yet. I don't even know how we can get into the pitch."

"Well, first things first. Let's get back and make sure you don't get fired. At least for another few weeks."

"Gee, thanks."

Jimmy wanders over with our change.

"What are you two up to? I've never seen the both of you so serious."

"Nothing much. Just trying to save our stupid agency from crashing and burning."

He sits with us.

"Anything I can do to help?"

"We need a war room, Jimmy. We need a room where we can come up with a pitch outside of the agency."

"A war room? How about the private room I have upstairs?"

"Don't you need that for parties?"

"How long do you need it for?"

"A week and a half."

"No problem. I've got nothing on the schedule for three weeks."

"Really? That would be great!"

"It's even got Internet connections."

"Fantastic. But let me ask you a question. Why are you doing this?"

Jimmy looks at his hands and then stares off for a bit.

"Peter Vine is one of the best people I ever met in my life. He used to come in here by himself when his demons got too bad. We'd talk about things that we never talked about with anyone else.

"He was the one who lent me the money to buy this place.

No strings attached. 'Pay it back when you can,' he said. And I did. Some months I paid him $25. He never complained.

"That was a long time ago, and I paid him back every cent. I love the man, and it pisses me off so much what they did to him.

"I won't even let Drew in the place. He came in once, and I asked him to leave. Told him he wasn't welcome. So I know you guys are up to something, and I figure it's probably good for H&V, whatever it is. So I'm glad to help anyway I can."

I'm speechless. Seems Vine has more friends than I realized.

"Thanks, Jimmy. We'll come over after work today and set things up."

We take off.

*   *

We walk as slowly as we can around the corner. My cell continues to buzz and vibrate, and I continue to ignore it. I'm dreading what I have to face, and Rach is dreading getting back to work on creative she despises.

We walk into the building.

"Once more, dear friends, into the breach."

We ride the elevator in silence. I get off first and head back into the vortex.

*   *

I finally look at my cell. Ramon has texted to confirm he'll meet me out front tonight at seven. I respond and confirm.

Kristina has texted and left a message asking again about hooking her up. Smiley. Smiley.

Bruce has left two messages telling me to find him before I speak to the trolls.

The bitch has texted to tell me that Don has surfaced and asks what she should do.

The ex has Tweeted.

Orchids. Orchids. Orchids. Custom for me.

When I get to my desk, my message light is blinking, and I have forty-seven new e-mails. High priority from troll number one telling me that I must attend a meeting at 3:00 PM with himself and troll number two. I click that I'll attend. Seems I'm the only attendee.

An e-mail from Ange responding to my troll alert that I've misconstrued several facts of the matter and she'll be more than happy to provide additional information. Nice to see how quickly she's covering her ass and giving herself leeway to go either way. Chicken.

An e-mail from Bruce along the same lines. Keeping his options open. Playing the game. Throw me under the bus or defend me? Which way is the wind blowing? Another chicken.

And then the e-mail that breaks my heart and pisses me off so much I actually see stars.

It's from Chas to the Flake-Off team stating that, effective immediately, Marissa is no longer working for the company. No reason given. But I know. E-mail was sent only fifteen minutes ago.

I drop my mouse and run to the elevators.

*   *

I get off on 11 and head right toward Marissa's station. She sees me coming and, to my absolute surprise, gives me a big smile. She's packing her few personal items into her backpack.

"I can't believe this. Did you deny it like I told you to?"

"There really wasn't any point to that. They could just

look at the logs of my machine. Besides, everyone around here saw you here and saw you take off with the flash drive."

"I am so sorry."

"Don't be. I mean it. You've done me a favor. I think Chas and Ange and Drew are the biggest fools I've ever met in my life. I have absolutely hated working for them."

"I must say, you don't seem real upset."

"I came here to work for Vine. I loved it while he was here. Learned something every day. Now? It's just crappy work and untalented, petty bosses."

"I'm still sorry. No matter what, it was a paycheck."

"Listen, Ryan, you didn't make me give you that art. I wanted to give it to you. I thought you were doing the right thing. I'd do it again."

"How did Chas handle it?"

"I guess he wasn't so sick that he couldn't come in. He called me into Ange's office, and they said that I'd violated company policy by releasing unapproved art. They said we all have to be a team and I obviously wasn't a team player. They told me to pack my stuff and leave."

"He probably enjoyed it."

"Oh he did. He knows I think he's a jerk, and he's probably glad I gave him an excuse."

She's done packing, so we head toward the elevators. We head down together, and I walk with her out front.

"Listen. Rach and I have formed a conspiracy to hijack the Leary pitch. We have no idea how we're going to do it yet, but we're going to somehow."

"I hear the concepts and creative are god awful."

"So word's already out, huh?"

"Only among the connected crowd."

"So here's the deal. We're setting up our own war room over at Ar. Jimmy's totally with us. We can use all the help we can get."

"I'm in. I'm totally in. Besides, I've got some extra time on my hands."

We laugh and she gives me a hug.

"Might as well head over there and get set up. What can I do?"

"It would be great if you could start filling up a wall with as many competitive ads as you can find. Also start printing out commentaries and opinions on fashion trends from the experts. But also start checking the blogs and less well-known fashionistas. I'd also like to track what labels celebrities are wearing and also who's pitching for whom."

"Is that all?"

"For now."

"What do I tell Jimmy?"

"Tell him the secret password is now Vine. All others are to be shot on sight."

She heads off and I go back inside. It's two thirty. Thirty minutes to troll time.

*   *

When I get off on my floor, I see that Bruce is actually sitting at my desk waiting for me.

"Look who decided to show up."

"Listen, Bruce, I just did what you told me to do."

"Well, not exactly. But that's beside the point at this point."

"I'm meeting with the trolls at three o'clock."

"Oh I know. I've spoken to Ange, and we both decided that this is between you and Chas. You've declared war on each other, and either one of you will win or you'll both lose. We don't really care."

"In other words, I'm on my own."

"You're on your own."

"Well thanks, Bruce. Again, it's so nice to know you have my back."

"Kid, one of these days maybe you'll learn that in this business, nobody has your back."

I hate it when he calls me kid.

*   *

I sit and start breezing through my e-mail to kill another fifteen minutes. Just the usual stuff. I get through all my new messages and then make my way through my voice mail. Nothing critical. But the message from Marissa saying good-bye from before I saw her gets me all pumped up again. Chas is going down.

It's five minutes to three and time to go. I head to the elevators and get off on 17, home to senior management and the accountants, lawyers, and compliance folks. Almost as much fun as the creative floor.

I find conference room 1704 and am just about to open the door when Chas comes out. He gives me a big smile, says nothing, and heads off.

Great. They got his story first.

I head in. Bill and Carlos, a.k.a. troll one and troll two, are waiting for me in their white shirts and 1980s ties. Bill's tie is stained. You have to look close, as the marinara sauce is close in color to the tie itself. Both are a bit chubby and have little teeth that make them look like piranhas. They live for situations like this.

Bill motions for the chair.

"Please, Ryan, have a seat. Would you like a soda?" He points to the credenza. Free sodas were banned months ago. But not up here on 17.

"No thanks."

"Then let's get started, shall we? These are rather disturbing allegations that you've made here."

I say nothing. Just like court. Answer the question, but don't give up anything you don't have to.

"You claim in your e-mail that the photographer Chas suggested was his girlfriend."

"He didn't 'suggest' her. He insisted for over a week that we use her and refused to show us any other photographers."

"Perhaps he felt very strongly about it. It is a creative decision."

"Standard procedure is for us to get three bids."

"True, but there are exceptions if the creative department feels that a particular resource is necessary for a given project."

"Well, that's interesting, as she had never done any hair care work or any packaged goods work prior to this shoot."

"Chas also claims that Ms. Greene is not his girlfriend."

I have to give Chas credit. That is pretty slick.

"Then I guess sleeping with someone and living with them for the last nine months doesn't qualify as a girlfriend. It sounds like a girlfriend to me. And I do seem to recall them together at the holiday party. There were even pictures. But what do I know?"

"If you knew that Chas was violating company policy, why didn't you tell us or tell your boss, Bruce Winters?

"Like I said in my e-mail, I didn't want to be a rat. And because Chas insisted that she was really good. I wanted to be a team player."

"I'm sure. And then today you violated company policy by making a graphic designer give you a copy of unapproved art, which you then took to the client without someone from the creative department present."

"That's pretty funny because no one from the creative department has come with me to present Flake-Off creative for the last six months. I've begged them to come with me, and they're always too busy."

"So you've been violating company policy for the last six months?"

I'm starting to feel like Alice.

"I would view it a bit differently and say that the creatives are violating policy by not coming with me, but that's just me."

"No need to be impertinent, Mr. Simmons."

Now it's Mr. Simmons. I decide to take off the gloves.

"As a matter of fact, Bill, I informed you via e-mail the first time it happened, and I don't seem to recall ever getting a reply from you. Would you like me to resend you the e-mail? I do archive all my e-mails. I'd be happy to find it for you."

"That won't be necessary."

Now Carlos pipes up.

"Now about the budget for this project. I'd like you to explain how you planned on covering the added retouching costs."

"I negotiated a reduction in fees from the photographer, and I was going to borrow the rest from another budget line."

"I don't seem to recall seeing a revised project estimate from you reflecting such a change."

"Well that's right, Carlos, I was going to update you in our next project budget meeting next week."

"I appreciate that, Mr. Simmons, but for changes over 2 percent of the budget, you're supposed to let me know right away so that I can plan and forecast accordingly."

"Well that's interesting, Carlos, because this has happened about twenty-five times in the past, and you've never asked me to update you outside of the project budget meetings, but I'll be happy to do so on a going-forward basis."

And we're back to Bill.

"Well, thank you for your time, Mr. Simmons. We're going to review what we've heard, and we'll let you know if there are any next steps required."

"Well thanks, guys, but I have a question for you."

They seem surprised, as they're used to asking the questions. Their eyebrows go up as one.

"So what am I supposed to do about the unnecessary shoot that Chas has scheduled for tomorrow?"

Bill smiles.

"Well, that's between you and Chas, now isn't it? We don't make creative decisions."

I smile back.

"That will be all, Mr. Simmons."

*   *

I head back to my cube. Before I can even look at my e-mail, Nate is lurking over my wall.

"I'm in."

It takes me a minute, but then I get it.

"You hacked eDating?"

"Shhhh. Not so loud. I could get arrested for this shit."

He smiles and motions for me to follow him. We head back toward the far end of the floor where the techies hang out. They've carved out their own area where others fear to tread.

Nate uses his card to enter their domain. I've always loved it back here. There's all kinds of equipment in various stages of breakdown, and wires and cables all over the place, and in the corner is a small, sealed-off room, which is kept frigid, that houses our servers.

We go over to Nate's corner, which can only be described as a mini command center. Nate can pretty much do what he wants. Senior management hates dealing with the guts of technology, so he has more free rein than he probably should. But Nate's also wicked efficient, and he runs a smooth department and gets shit done. He keeps everything running and sticks to his budget, so he's pretty much left alone. His staff loves him, and he keeps them happy.

I sit down in the chair he wheels over and watch him do his magic.

"So I figured out a way around their firewalls, and I can now pretty much access their profiles. I'm staying well away from their payment system, where things are much more secure."

"So have you looked at the bitch's account yet?"

"Sure have. She's been spending hours looking at her matches and trying to communicate with them. This has got to be one horny, desperate lady."

"She's been communicating with some guy named Don. Can you see that?"

"Yup, here it is. Don Carter."

"So could you—theoretically of course—pretend to be someone in the system and make up communications between them?"

"Now that I'm in, it's a piece of cake."

We smile.

"I'll get back to you."

He waves as I take off.

"Toodles."

*   *

I finally get back to my desk and check my e-mail. Just as I expected. There's an e-mail from Chas confirming the shoot with everyone. I decide to play the game, hit Reply All, and start writing. I decide to include the trolls on the cc list for the fun of it.

> All—
>   Please note that this shoot and the
> related budget have not been approved
> by the account team or by the client. The
> client has already approved the prior shots

and is expecting to receive layouts with them incorporated by this Monday, per the original project schedule.

The account team will not approve any invoices that result from this shoot, and we expect to have layouts for the client per the schedule.

Please let me know if you have any further questions on this issue.

Ryan

I hit Send. Oh, the glory of a paper trail. We'll see if Chas has the guts to go ahead with the shoot.

But for now, I don't care. It's four thirty, and I decide I've had enough. I'll head over to Jimmy's before I have to meet Ramon.

*   *

Jimmy smiles when I enter and points me upstairs. At the top and to the right is a decent-size room that's normally used for private parties. Marissa has been a whirlwind. She's all set up at a table for four with her laptop and two monitors. At least twenty-five magazines have been torn to pieces, and all of the fashion ads have been tacked up onto a wall. She's got a stack of printouts on the table next to her that look like various reports and white papers she's hunted down on the Web regarding fashion trends and the major designers.

I give Marissa a huge smile and head over and give her a hug.

"I've had more fun in the last few hours than I've had in the last two years!"

"I can't believe how much you've done! This is great. I was

beginning to feel like this was mission impossible, and now I feel like maybe we can do something."

"Great, now shut up and start reading."

She hands me the stack of reports. Jimmy appears and leaves an ice-cold Stella next to me. It's nice to have friends. I start reading.

*   *

I get though a good number of reports and have a bite to eat before I have to head out to meet Ramon. I've texted Rach and told her to stop by. She'll be excited.

I've purposely avoided checking my e-mail and voice mail. I'm more interested in trying to figure out what adventure Ramon has in store for me tonight than I am in predicting what Chas will do.

I hit the front at exactly seven o'clock, and ten seconds later Ramon appears. I'm genuinely glad to see him. We make our greetings, and I follow him west.

We hit Central Park and wander our way across to the west side.

"So I hear Miss Kristina is trying to hunt down your ass."

"I wish it was my ass she was after. She just wants to star with Alexi in those vodka ads."

"Dougie tells me you're a failure as a gay man."

"Oh, big-time. I played to every stereotype in the book."

"But it was good enough for the real girls."

"I owe you for that."

"Don't you worry. I'm running a tab. You're gonna owe ol' Ramon your firstborn by the time we're done."

We exit the park on the west side and head down into the subway. We're heading uptown.

*   *

We get off at 125th Street. Harlem. It's a beautiful night, and the streets are fairly crowded.

"We're going hunting, my friend. We're hunting the most elusive of all creatures. The so-called urban youth, who will define the coming waves of what will be cool and hip next season. The arbiters of fashion, right before your eyes."

I laugh out loud.

"You sound like a bad voiceover for a fashion documentary."

"I'll take that as a compliment. But I'm serious. We're gonna spend a few hours up here meeting kids. Black kids, Hispanic kids, kids of every possible combination of minority. These kids have no money to speak of, but they have a fashion sense that can't be kept down. These kids are cooler than any of those old stick-up-their-ass designers downtown who think they know what's what. So keep your eyes open. The stuff you see here will be the stuff in the magazines next year and the year after."

"We going anywhere in particular?"

"Oh you bet we are. We're going back to high school."

"High school?"

*   *

We turn off 125th Street and head up Columbus for two blocks. We head toward the entrance to JFK High School. One line of the outdoor bulletin board reads, "Thursday—Varsity Men's B Ball Regional Finals."

There is a very definite buzz in the air—the buzz of high school sports and teenage hormones. I can feel it and smell it as soon as we enter the building. We pay our $5 and head in. The game is late in the second quarter with a close score. The gymnasium 's packed, the cheerleaders are cheering, the coaches are yelling, and the crowd is roaring.

As usual, Ramon is well known, and receives a constant flow of greetings as we find a place to sit in the bleachers.

"This is where I went to high school. I'm still somewhat of a legend here."

"Why am I not surprised? Basketball?"

"Oh yeah. We made it to the state finals. I also come up here a few times a month to mentor a few kids."

"Mr. Ramon—what is your last name anyway?"

"Diaz. Ramon Diaz."

"Well Mr. Diaz, you do surprise me."

"I love these kids. I love coming up here."

We watch for a while.

"So listen, here's the deal. Once again, you watch and learn. These games are a key component of social life up here. They can't have dances because they always end in fights. They hang in the streets, but it's dangerous. These games can get ugly too, but look around and you'll see a pretty strong police presence. It's relatively safe here, and the parents know it.

"Like I said, these kids don't have a lot of money, so they have to get creative. The clothes they wear are all they got to define themselves. Even the tough guys go out of their way to maintain a look while pretending that they don't care.

"All the big trends start up here. Or in Watts, or the South Side of Chicago. Look around and you'll start to see some new shit. Check out those girls over there. They probably made those skirts themselves. Big, bright, bold, sexy, and primitive. They call it 'tribal.' My guess is it's gonna be huge by next spring. They actually use the Web to research the clothing worn by the ancient tribes of Africa and then figure out ways to modernize it.

"The good designers are up here all the time. There's probably a few here right now. The ones like Leary are nowhere to be found. They think they know better, they think that they can dictate the trends instead of letting them emerge. You ask me, that's why they're getting killed.

"Now check out those wannabee gangbangers over there. They've already moved on from the lowriders with their boxers hanging out. Among these kids, that's already old, old, old. See the military influence sneaking into their pants? They've all got older brothers and sisters coming home from Iraq, and those siblings are leaving behind their older uniforms. And it's cool again to serve.

"Now look at their shoes. You still see the oversized basketball shoes for those that can afford them, but a lot of them are wearing military boots, again from siblings coming home. Marines are the hottest. Or actually, special forces, of course. Then comes army. Air force are too rare to have much impact. Navy don't do boots."

I just take it all in and watch the game at the same time. The buzzer goes off for the half, with the home team down by two as the final shot of the half goes wide. The crowd groans. The teams head off the court, and the crowd starts moving toward the restrooms and the refreshment stands.

"Let's go talk to some kids. I'm gonna introduce you as a big swinging dick advertising guy up here looking to learn about fashion."

"That's perfectly true."

"Yeah, except for the big swinging dick part. C'mon."

The next fifteen minutes blow my mind. The kids obviously adore Ramon, and a small crowd gathers around us where we're sitting out in front of the school. I get smart and take out my phone and start videoing the kids as they talk.

What's crystal clear is that these kids can't afford the high-end designers, but they know them inside out. They've got an opinion on everything, from the classic to the up-and-coming. And they all want into the scene. They want to be models or designers. They want to open boutiques and Web sites and sell their own stuff.

And they think they smell opportunity when it comes to me. They assume that I can get them into commercials. They want to show me their designs. They want my phone number, want to know where I work. These kids are not shy.

And once again, the news is grim for Leary. These kids laugh and say they "don't want none of that Muffy and Buffy bullshit."

I probe to get beyond the bravado and the posing in front of their friends. It takes a bit, but the main thing that comes through is that these kids love the process. They don't want to just go to the store and buy stuff. They want to be part of it.

The game is about to resume, and the kids head back into the gym.

Ramon and I walk a few blocks and then head into a small coffeehouse called Uptown Momma's and sit at the counter.

"Let's grab some dessert. Momma's has the best pie in all Harlem, probably the whole city. Maybe the whole world."

I order coffee and pecan pie. Ramon goes for cherry.

Momma herself comes out from the kitchen with our pie. She sets the plates down, and Ramon gets off his stool to give her a big hug.

"Ramon!"

"Momma."

Momma is probably ninety-five years old, but she could pass for seventy. Her eyes miss nothing.

"So who's this cute white boy coming to taste my pie?"

I step forward and give her my hand.

"Momma, this is Ryan Simmons, and I'm trying real hard to teach him about life. And life just ain't worth living without your pie."

"Now that's the truth."

Momma nods toward a table and gets herself some coffee from behind the counter. The three of us sit, and Ramon and I dig into our pie.

I've always liked pecan pie, but after one bite, I realize that what I thought was pecan pie was just a poor imitation.

Momma sees the look on my face and smiles. She's seen the look before.

"Ramon, can you give us a minute?"

"Sure, Momma."

He heads back toward the counter.

"You got a lot on your mind, young man."

I look up into her eyes.

"Now that's the truth."

She laughs.

"I'm in way over my head. I'm trying to do something that I have no right to be doing."

"Oh, you got a right to be doing it. Seems to me, though, that you may have to lose a battle or two in order to win the war."

Chas. How can losing to Chas possibly help me? And how the hell does she know so much?

"I'm not sure I understand."

"Sometimes you don't have to understand, just trust."

You ever have one of those moments when you just stop and say, "What am I doing here?" This is one of those moments. What am I doing sitting at Uptown Momma's eating a piece of delicious pecan pie with an ancient black lady on a Thursday night?

"You have no idea how much I need to beat this guy."

"You don't have to beat him. He doesn't matter."

I finish my pie, and despite everything weighing on my mind, my tummy sure feels good.

"There's someone you have to speak to."

I assume she's talking about someone at the coffee shop. I look around.

"No, no one here. Nobody I know. Somebody you know."

I probably look a bit lost.

"Someone who can help you. You'll figure it out."

Ramon wanders over.

"You ready to hit the road?"

We say our good-byes to Momma and head outside. I start laughing.

"I feel like I just met the Oracle from *The Matrix*!"

"Yeah, except ol' Momma's for real."

"Don't you start going all Morpheus on me. I can't take that right now."

"What she said, it was for you alone."

"No, no, stop, please stop."

"Guns. We need guns. Lots of guns."

*   *

Ramon and I split up at the subway station. He tells me that I've got the night off tomorrow, but he'll see me at Paul's party. He's still laughing his head off, imitating Morpheus and Neo.

I've got a long ride home. I pop my e-mail to my cell before I go into the subway so I can read it on the way. I head down onto the platform to wait.

But first I skim through my texts—another from Kristina, and one from Rach. Kristina is one persistent thing, isn't she? Rach has actually sent me three messages, as she ran out of characters. She tells me that Marissa is amazing and that they've got a ton of great stuff for me to look at. She says they're both planning on spending the weekend in the war room.

Nice to know I've got a cavalry behind me, motley though it may be.

It's time to check my e-mail and see if Chas the wonder boy has responded to my e-mail. Yup. I click to open it.

> All—
>   Please note that tomorrow's shoot is a go! I repeat, a go! Need I remind certain

team members that we are a *creative* agency,
and when there are disagreements, we must
always put our best creative efforts forward.

I have reviewed the entire situation with
Drew, and he is in complete agreement.
There's always a way to handle budget
issues, if we all just pull together as a team.

See you all tomorrow—coffee and
donuts are on me!

Chas

I sure hope Momma Oracle is right, 'cause this particular
battle is already lost.

I've had enough for one day. I'm going home. I'm going
to bed.

*   *

Pitch Minus 6 Days—Friday

It's Friday. I treat myself to a nice breakfast at a diner a few blocks from the office. Two eggs over easy, ham, english muffin, short stack on the side, at least four refills on the coffee.

I could head down to watch the shoot, just for the fun of it, but take a pass. I head into the building and up to my floor.

I boot up and open my Outlook. How best to tell the bitch that my agency has lost its mind? That we decided to overrule her approval and spend more money and waste more time on a stupid dandruff ad that no one cares about anyway?

Whoa, Bessie.

How about, "Good news! We're going to make the Flake-Off ad absolutely spectacular! We here at H&V are so committed to creative excellence that we don't bother listening to our clients. And here's an invoice for $10,000."

Or maybe, "Chas's girlfriend threatened to break up with him if he didn't break all of our rules and hire her for your shoot. Then after she totally screwed it up, he decided to pay her twice, just so she could mess it up all over again. Oh well, at least he probably got laid. Too bad you have to pay for it!"

I save my drafts and decide it needs more thought. I'm usually pretty damn good at spinning lemons into lemonade, but this time I'm at a total loss.

Nate saunters up just in time to save me from further contemplation.

"So now that we're in, what's the plan?"

"Well, believe it or not, the plan is to try and make the bitch happy so that she leaves me in peace."

"That's no fun."

"Oh, ye of little faith."

I get up and follow Nate back to his lair. I roll a chair over next to him.

"What we need to do is figure out all the women who our buddy Don is flirting with. Then we have to pretend to be them and systematically blow him off until he's forced back to our lady in waiting."

"You are a sick, sick man. I like it."

I get up to leave. Nate is already writing a search string to figure out everyone Don is speaking with. I leave him to his fun.

*   *

I head back to my cube. Oh joy. Bruce is waiting for me. He nods for me to follow him to his office.

I follow him in and sit as he closes the door.

"So why aren't you down at the shoot?"

"Please tell me you're kidding."

"It's your account. It's your budget. It's your responsibility to be there to make sure everything goes okay."

"Consider it my one-man protest."

"You've let this whole thing get way out of hand, Ryan."

"You know what? That's bullshit, Bruce. I've been putting up with Chas's crap for almost a year now. You should be helping me. You should be backing me up. Chas should be fired, and you know it."

"Chas doesn't work for me."

"Why didn't you tell Ange or Drew that this whole thing was crazy? I don't have the clout to go up against them, but you do."

"Have you discussed this with your client yet?"

"No, I haven't. I've had to make up shit and lie through my teeth to her to cover for Chas and his team for months. But even I, the master of spin, haven't figured out how to explain this one."

I get up and start out.

"Let me know if you have ideas on how to get out of this one. That I'd appreciate."

I'm gone.

✳   ✳

I get back to my desk and start wading through my real work. Flake-Off actually has a rather aggressive plan for this year, and it's time to start fleshing out all the details. Two more commercials to be shot, media plan for the third and fourth quarters, response analysis on the coupon drops—I've got plenty to keep me busy.

I pop up the explanation e-mail a few times and try to write it, but no great insights have struck. Sometimes, it just doesn't make sense to even try to put lipstick on the pig. This pig is too big and mean and ugly.

It's late morning by now. My cell rings. It's Dave, one of my moles in the creative department. Dave's an intern—lower than a peon. He must be down at the shoot.

"Ryan."

"Ry, you won't believe it. I wish you were here to see this."

"What, what's going on? Talk to me."

Dave is cracking up.

"You won't believe it. It's an absolute thing of beauty. Chas and his non-girlfriend girlfriend had a massive fight. I'm talking yelling at the top of their lungs and practically throwing things."

"This, Dave, is living proof why there are company policies."

He is cracking up.

"Dave, stay with me here. Is anything getting done?"

"Not really. The models that Amy and Chas picked don't look anything like their headshots. They must not have ever met them. So they started fighting about that. They finally decide to use the least unattractive of the two. And then Amy can't get the lighting right, so they start fighting about that. Before you know it, she's calling him a wuss for not standing up to you, and he calls her a bitch and tells her to shut up, and she storms off, and he goes after her, and they close the door, and she's telling him that he's an asshole and wants to break up with him, and we're all standing around listening, and man, it was beautiful."

"How'd it end up?"

"She left. Just took off. We're all sitting around, eating Chas's donuts and waiting for him to tell us what to do."

"You know what the best part is?"

"What's that?"

"It will all be my fault."

"Not this time, Ry."

"What do you mean?"

"Check your e-mail in a few seconds. I videotaped the whole thing with my phone. Just sent it to you."

It pays to have friends in low places.

"Dave, have I told you recently that I love you?"

"I'd say you owe me, but helping to embarrass Chas is all the payment I need."

"Does he know you taped it?"

"He has no clue. He was much too busy."

"Sweet. No matter what you say, I owe you. Later, buddy."

"Later."

Sure enough, Dave's e-mail arrives with a 5-meg attachment. I forward it to my Gmail account for safekeeping and then click on the attachment, making sure to turn my volume down first.

This is better than porn. It's everything Dave said it was and more. Now I get to have fun watching to see how Chas will spin it up the ladder, knowing that I can call him on it at any time. I decide not to e-mail the bitch until I see how this is going to play out.

I check my Gmail to make sure it's there and then also copy the file to a flash drive. Just for fun viewing at my convenience, I also e-mail it to my cell. Then I delete Dave's e-mail as well as the forwarded e-mail from my Sent file.

I remember what Momma Oracle told me, but it's still nice to have options.

I look up, and to my delight, Rach is approaching. I figure she's here to drag me off to lunch. I'm only too happy to comply.

*   *

I tell Rach about the fight down at the shoot as we head out of the building toward Ar. Then I tell her about the video, which I let her watch on my phone. Trust me, it's just as much fun the second time around.

Rach is staring at my phone aghast and laughing at the same time. It's amusing to watch her facial muscles try to do the right thing in accordance with her emotions.

"Amazing, huh?"

"Amazing. Have you heard anything else since? Has she come back?"

"Haven't heard. I can check with Dave again soon, but I'm sure he'd let me know if things have changed."

"So now what are you going to tell your client?"

"No clue. I think I'm just going to see how it plays out later today or Monday."

"You should put that video on YouTube and send the link out to everyone at the agency."

"We'll see. But that's a great idea. You're worse than me."

She takes my arm and we walk the next few blocks in silence.

*   *

We get to Ar, say hi to Jimmy, and head upstairs. Marissa

smiles and then introduces us to a tall, lanky kid with a bunch of tattoos and piercings.

"This is Jeremy. I met him at night school. He's a wiz at numbers, so I hired him as an intern."

That gets a good laugh out of all of us.

"He's going through all of the public filings for Leary and putting together a financial picture for you."

"Awesome. Nice to meet you Jeremy. Welcome to the team."

"Hey."

Rach and I shake hands with him while Marissa continues.

"There's a stack of stuff for you to read. I weeded out what I thought was the more important stuff."

"Thanks, Marissa, this is great."

Jimmy comes in with a platter of burgers and fries. I grab a seat and a burger and start making my way through Marissa's articles.

*   *

I'm lost in the research when I realize that it's already three o'clock. Rach headed back about an hour ago. I call Dave.

"Hey, Ryan."

"What's doing?"

"I'm back at the office. We all waited about another hour and then bagged it and came back. Amy never came back. Neither did Chas."

"Roger that. Thanks, man."

I click off. I'm truly wondering what Chas is going to do. I check my e-mail. Nothing from him. I decide I better head back.

As I walk back to the office, I let my mind wander over Leary and everything that's been jammed into my mind over the last week. I'm exhausted but exhilarated at the same time.

But nothing has truly clicked yet. Tumblers are spinning around in my brain, but they haven't locked onto a solid concept, insight, or approach.

I'm hoping that going out tonight and getting really smashed might be just the thing. Maybe I'll take off early. Maybe Rach will join me. Maybe there really is a Santa Claus.

As soon as I approach my cube, I know that I'm not leaving early. I'm not going out to get smashed. And there most definitely is no Santa Claus, Easter Bunny, or Great Pumpkin.

Bruce's assistant, MaryAnn, is sitting at my desk waiting for me. She's a sweet, mousy type, and she actually looks scared.

"You're supposed to come with me up to the eleventh floor right away."

"The eleventh floor?"

"Yes. Drew's conference room. Bruce is waiting for you up there."

"Do you know why?"

"Something to do with the Flake-Off shoot."

Now there's a big surprise.

"Anything more specific?"

"I really don't know, Ry. I wish I knew more. I really do. We better go."

I follow her toward the elevators. This should be fun.

*　　　*

We get off on 11 and head toward the corner. Drew refused to take Vine's old office up on 17—thought it was bad luck and decided it would be "better for the troops" if he was down on the same floor with them. It was more likely so that he could keep his eyes on them.

His corner office is pretty huge, with a great view facing

downtown. He has his own conference room next door, where Bruce is waiting, reading some documents. MaryAnn scoots out behind me, and I take a seat.

"Hey, Bruce. What's this about?"

"I think we're about to get our asses chewed out."

At least he said we.

"Have you already spoken to him?"

"Nope. But I know all about what happened at the shoot."

"You mean the nonshoot?"

He chuckles.

"Yeah, something like that."

I don't have much respect for Bruce, but he hates Drew as much as anyone, and sometimes he rises to the occasion. We'll have to see how this plays out. He could just as easily throw me under the bus.

Drew loves to keep people stewing. We sit for a good ten minutes before Drew breezes into the room followed by Chas.

I should probably keep my mouth shut, but I decide to go on the offensive.

"Hey, Chas. How'd the shoot go?"

They both ignore me and sit down. Drew glares at us.

"You must be Simmons."

"You can call my Ryan."

"So what do you have to say for yourself?"

"I don't follow."

"You are the account exec on Flake-Off, are you not?"

"I am."

"So why weren't you at the shoot today supporting your creative team?"

"I wasn't at the shoot because the shoot was unnecessary, as the client already approved the prior shots. I indicated as much in an e-mail yesterday. Chas then overruled me and went ahead anyway. I made it clear that there was no budget for the shoot. I didn't attend, as I did not approve the budget."

"Since when do you approve creative budgets?"

"I don't specifically approve creative budgets, but I do have overall responsibility for keeping our expenses within client-approved budgets."

"Listen, you little shit. I'm tired of hearing your name come up all the time from Chas. He's your creative director. Maybe you should learn to listen to him."

"Should I listen to him when he breaks company policy?"

"What are you talking about?"

"He insisted that we use his girlfriend as the photographer on the shoot."

"You signed off on her."

"Yes, I did, and I already took responsibility for that mistake by telling finance and compliance."

"So this whole fiasco is in fact your fault."

"Let me get this straight. Chas over here breaks company policy by even recommending that we use his girlfriend. When I say no, he has a hissy fit and insists that we use her, promising me that she's really talented and has done lots of this type of work. He also refuses to get two other bids, as per company policy. I finally relent because we're out of time. Then it turns out that his girlfriend has no talent, and she insists that we use her zit-infested brother as the model for the shoot. I try to force them to get another model, but both she and Chas insist that we use him. This after I begged for two days to see the models they were recommending.

"So now the photos of zit face need massive retouching, which is not budgeted. We figure a way around that, and Marissa totally rocks out and makes the photos look great, for which you then fire her. Meanwhile, back at the ranch, the client is screaming bloody murder for the shots, so I run them over, without Chas, who is out sick but apparently not too sick to come in and fire Marissa. The client likes the shots and approves them.

"But Chas still insists on reshooting because his girlfriend is mad that I made her reduce her fee because she lied about her past experience and totally screwed up the shoot.

"So Chas decides to go ahead anyway, after I made it clear in writing that there was no budget and the client had already approved the shots."

I turn to Chas.

"And now I hear that the shoot didn't even happen because you had a massive fight with your girlfriend and you both stormed off. And somehow this is all my fault?"

Chas, a bit red in the face, starts screaming at me.

"That's bullshit. The shoot was cancelled because the photographer said she hadn't received written approval from the account team."

"You're telling me it's not because you had a massive fight with her."

"Never happened. There was no fight."

I reach for my cell to show the video, but Momma Oracle's warning pops into my head. I decide to trust her, even if I'm not sure why.

"Okay, Chas. Whatever you say."

Drew points at Bruce.

"Get your people in line, Bruce, or I'll do it for you. One more screwup by this asshole, and I'll make sure he gets fired. I don't need this crap from your puny accounts while I'm working on a pitch to save this place. And neither does Chas!"

Bruce stands.

"Those puny accounts are paying your salary right now, Drew. Yours too, Chas. And as far as I recall, you struck out on your last two pitches to save the place. Let's hope you don't make it oh for three."

Bruce pushes me toward the door and we leave.

Hmmm. Maybe wimpy ol' Bruce has some balls after all.

*   *

As soon as we get on the elevator, Bruce unleashes.

"That pompous asshole. How dare he threaten my people. Only I get to threaten my people."

"You don't really think I'm wrong about this, do you?"

"Of course not."

"Do me a favor on this. Get Chas to confirm to you in an e-mail what he just said—that there was no fight down at the shoot."

"Why?"

"I can't tell you right now, but you'll be glad you did."

He looks at me funny, but I know he'll do it.

*   *

I get back to my cube, and Nate is waiting for me.

"Operation Mistletoe is underway."

"You're having too much fun with this."

"I am. I figured the best way to do it was to pretend to be Don, and then do weird things to scare away the women he's been flirting with."

"I hope you're being careful. You don't want to get him kicked off the site."

"Way ahead of you, Ry, way ahead of you."

"How many so far?"

"One yesterday, and one today."

"How many are we talking about?"

"Ol' Don has been quite the Don Juan. He had ten women on the line. And now he's down to eight. He'll be all alone by the end of the weekend."

"So with any luck, the bitch should hear from him by Monday."

"That would be the plan."

"Carry on, my good man, carry on."

*   *

Nate heads back to his important work, and I sit at my desk, staring into space.

My cell buzzes with a text message. It's Kristina again. I'm starting to admire her.

Alexi—small party Sunday night at my place. Please, please tell me you can come.

What the hell.

No promises, but I will try. Address? Time?

She texts back the info with a bunch of smiley faces.

I look up and there is Rach. She seems a bit down. She holds up a flash drive.

"Wait till you see this crap. Let's head over to Jimmy's."

I've certainly had enough for one day. I shut down and we head out.

*   *

I tell her about the meeting with Drew and Chas on the way over.

"Way to go Bruce. Who would have thought it?"

"Yeah, he's actually more protective of his people than I thought. It's a relief to know that if I get fired, he feels strongly that it should be him doing it instead of Drew."

We laugh.

"Do you think this whole thing we're doing is pointless?"

I think about it.

"No. I don't. We'd feel much worse if we did nothing. And something is going to pop."

"What I'm struggling with is how are we going to get to

present it anyway? Even if we come up with something, Drew will never even look at it, much less agree to include it."

"I know."

"So?"

"So we figure out a way to go around him. We talk to Jack himself. We call Duke Owen. We get weapons and hijack the meeting. We take Drew and Chas hostage the night before."

"I feel much better now."

"We're going to find a way because we have to. We're going to come up with a great idea because we have to."

"I believe you. I don't know why, but I believe you."

She leans in and squeezes me. Ah, for life's little pleasures.

*   *

We head into Ar and notice that Jimmy's day guy is behind the bar. We go upstairs and see that Jimmy is sitting with Jeremy. He's got his glasses on, something I've never seen before.

When Rach and I walk in, everyone looks up and waves.

Jeremy wanders over.

"Hey, Ry. Jimmy and I are ready to brief you on the numbers for Leary."

"Great."

I look at Jimmy.

"Since when are you a finance guy?"

"There is much you don't know about me."

Rach and I take a seat at a table, and Jeremy lays out a bunch of spreadsheets.

"So the news for Leary is pretty bad. We've gone through all of their filings for the last several years. First off, their stock has been declining slowly but surely. It's down 15 percent over the last three years. Revenues have declined steadily as well.

"Their businesses are off globally, not just the States.

It seems like they're getting cherry-picked left and right by upstarts and in their core businesses by the other big guys. This is despite the fact that they've increased their advertising by over 5 percent each year over the same period.

"Not surprisingly, they don't break out their numbers by brand. But all of them are declining except one small bright spot in Asia. They bought a very young designer's line there that has taken off; they're thinking about bringing the line to the U.S.

"That's the top line. I've attached a few pages here with much more detail for you to look over."

He hands me a stack of at least fifty pages.

"This is amazing work, Jeremy."

"Jimmy helped a ton—he knows his way around a 10-Q like you wouldn't believe."

They head back to their computers, and Marissa comes over.

"I've got some great stuff to take you through."

This is so cool. I feel like the CEO getting his weekly briefings. I could get used to this.

"Whatcha got?"

"There's a ton going on right now. Fashion is a truly crazy, difficult business. There are huge risks and huge rewards. You hit it right, you can't keep up with demand. You hit it wrong, and retailers are sending the crap back.

"As you know, Leary is into everything—clothing, accessories, cosmetics, watches, jewelry, fragrances, the works. They're also big into linens and even furniture.

"Each brand or designer label does its own marketing, and the efforts are somewhat all over the place. This is okay, because trying to do one unified effort would be much too generic to fit everything.

"The core Leary line has depended on the country club, old money, somewhat Waspy imagery for decades and decades. And for the most part, it's worked. It's been one of those labels that you can't go wrong with, that you'll never be embarrassed by, but that hasn't been cutting it anymore."

I cut in.

"The kids uptown referred to it as 'that Muffy and Buffy bullshit.'"

"That about sums it up. Their core audience is shrinking, and the fringe audiences aren't buying the stuff anymore. You used to see the big-time celebrities wearing Leary all the time, but now they're all wearing their own labels or those of their celebrity friends."

She hands me another stack of reading material.

"What do you think the answer is?"

"That's your job, Kemo Sabe."

Rach has been right next to me, listening to everything. She remembers the flash drive.

"Hey, everyone. Gather round. Here's Drew's answer to Leary's problems."

She pops in the flash drive and opens up the files.

"Drew is going to present just one overall direction. First, of course, he'll give an overview of their business and its 'challenges.'"

"Overall, because he's such a wuss, he's going to keep the overview on a positive note. He's going to stress the power of their equity and then segue into the importance of maintaining but modernizing it."

She pops open one file at a time and clicks through the imagery without saying anything. She doesn't have to. I summarize.

"So his creative brilliance is to take Muffy and Buffy and Biff out of the country club and put them into more hip and modern places."

"Yup."

"Instead of realizing that Muffy and Buffy are the problem."

"Exactly."

"What an idiot."

"Has anyone on the team tried to talk him out of it?"

"Everyone's too scared they'll get fired."

"Has Halliday seen this crap?"

"He's seeing it all on Monday. But he won't go up against Drew. He was never the creative guy."

"And it'll be too late anyway."

"Probably part of Drew's plan."

Jeremy pipes up.

"That stuff really sucks. It's patronizing as hell. If I saw that crap, I'd never buy Leary."

"Well, Jeremy, I think you've summed it up better than I could."

They're all staring at me, waiting for me to give them the answer.

"I can't tell you how great this is. You guys are amazing. I honestly wish I had an answer right now, or a direction, an approach—I'd even settle for an insight or two. Instead, let me tell you what I've been up to this last week, and maybe something will start to gel."

I proceed to tell them about my adventures of the last week with Ramon. My posse of bartender, unemployed graphic designer computer whiz, punk kid financial genius, and inside spy illustrator listen intently.

My story ends up taking awhile to tell, as we're constantly interrupted by mugs of beer, dinner, much laughter, and even an interesting discussion or two.

My description of Dougie walking the runway, and my feeble attempts to imitate him, has everyone crying with laughter.

Toward the end, Jeremy asks me who I think Momma Oracle was talking about, who it is I need to speak to. I tell him that I have no idea.

*   *

Marissa has captured anything relevant on flip chart sheets, which she's hung around the room. Looking at them now, sitting alone in our war room after the rest of them have left, I realize how much I've taken in, in so little time.

I stay for an hour by myself, jotting down my own notes and bits and pieces of ideas.

I realize it's past midnight and decide to close up, head downstairs, thank Jimmy, and say good night.

I head home, wondering who in hell Momma was talking about.

*   *

Pitch Minus 5 Days—Saturday

We all agreed to meet back at the war room the next morning at ten. I get there pretty much on time, and Marissa and Rach are already there.

"Mornin'."

"Hey, Ry. Grab a bagel."

I do.

"Rach, what is Drew presenting as a digital strategy? I don't recall seeing very much."

"That's because there isn't much. What he has is a pretty pathetic 'upgrade' to the existing Web site."

"That's it? No real Web strategy? Mobile strategy? Social media? User-generated stuff?"

"Nope, nope, nope, and nope. We've been pressing him about it, but he says 'those are details that we can address after they buy into the overall strategy.'"

Marissa pipes up.

"Digital probably should *be* the strategy."

"Ya think? Rach, how much has Drew been through the research? Didn't they send over like a mountain of stuff?"

"Yeah, they did. One copy, nothing electronic, so it couldn't be shared around easily. He kinda skimmed through it and then had Chas give it to Miriam to go through. She spent a week with it and then sent him a summary, which he read and promptly ignored."

"Any way we can get our hands on it?"

"Nope. Miriam has it locked in her office, and she's as mean as they come. We call her the wicked witch."

"Can we steal it?"

"No way. Her office is locked all the time, and I think it's locked in a file cabinet in her locked office."

"That sucks. How about the summary she gave to Drew? Did he share that with the team?"

"Of course not. We just do as we're told. We're not allowed to think."

I wonder if I could con Miriam into letting me see it. No way.

Miriam is the head of research. She's probably in her midfifties, and she was probably very attractive in her day. She was extremely well liked and powerful when Vine was around. She then became more and more bitter, as Drew tended to ignore her and cut her budgets. Her staff is a quarter of what it used to be. I'm not surprised that she's become mean and ornery.

I've interacted with her a few times, and found her to be quite brilliant. Too bad Drew is wasting her talent.

Jeremy wanders in around eleven and immediately devours two bagels loaded with cream cheese. The guy weighs probably 120 pounds.

Even though I don't have an overall concept, there are things I know I'm going to need. And I want to make it look like I know what I'm doing.

"Jeremy, can you put together a few PowerPoint slides that tell the sordid tale of Leary's financials?"

"Sure thing."

"Make it pretty brutal. Tell it like it is."

"You got it."

"Marissa, can you make a few slides on what their competitors are doing? Make it big and bold."

"Okay."

Rach heads over and joins her.

"I'll help."

I start going through the stuff that Jeremy and Marissa have gathered for me.

Rach wanders over to me about an hour later. "Did I tell you that this reporter from *Advertising Weekly* keeps calling me?"

"I don't think you mentioned it."

"She's been real persistent. I don't know how she got my name or number, but she knows that I'm on the pitch team.

She's begging me to give her the inside story of what we're doing."

"Have you actually spoken to her?"

"Only when I picked up the phone once. I told her I couldn't talk and referred her to Halliday's office, like we're supposed to."

"What's her name?"

"Janice Stone."

"Yeah, I've seen her byline before. She's been writing the whole series about the pitch."

"You think we should let her in on our little secret?"

"Much too dangerous."

"It sure would make a great story."

"Only if we're successful. And right now we got nothing. Nada. Zip."

"We've got a great team. We've got a cool war room. We've got much more than we did the last time we had this conversation."

"This is true."

"How about this. Let's just take some pictures and video as we go along. Just in case."

"That's a great idea."

Rach smiles. She doesn't waste any time in grabbing her digital camera from her bag. She wanders around taking a few pictures of all of us and then the room itself.

*   *

Jeremy and Marissa take off around six o'clock. I run over to the dry cleaners and pick up my borrowed clothes. Rach changes for the evening while I'm gone. She looks incredible in a very short skirt and a tight top that accents her cleavage. I try not to stare.

"Hey. You look beautiful."

"Thanks, Ry. I'll meet you at the bar."

She heads down and I change. I remember that feeling from the other night—how good it feels to be dressed like a million bucks.

I go down and meet Rach at the bar. I get a huge smile from her and some whistles from Jimmy behind the bar. I sit down next to Rach, and a Stella magically appears. I turn to Jimmy.

"Tell me more about Peter Vine."

"I could tell Vine stories for hours."

"Pick your favorite. That's all we have time for."

Jimmy thinks for a minute, pours himself a scotch on the rocks, and leans forward.

"There was this one time. Peter comes in around eight o'clock one night. Place was pretty deserted. Must have been a Tuesday. This was years ago. He sits down on a stool and orders a vodka on the rocks. He looks like shit, like he's been up for a few days straight.

"Turns out that's pretty much the case. He tells me that he has a huge pitch the next day and he's got squat. No ideas, no concepts, no insights, no storyboards, nothing. It's not a huge project, but it's an entry to Philip Morris, one of the biggest advertisers in the world. Took Halliday two years to get in the door, and now Vine's gonna blow it big-time.

"He downs his vodka and asks for another. Then he tells me all about what he's done to come up with an idea. He tells me about the brainstorming, the meetings, the interviews with smokers—he's pulled all of his tricks, and he's still got nothing.

"I ask him if he's giving up. He tells me the meeting is at 9:00 AM and it's 8:00 the night before. He tells me that he won't give up until 8:59 tomorrow morning. Then he'll go in and try to make up something on the spot, and if he can't, then he'll give up.

"Then he says, 'But for the next hour, and for the next few

drinks, I give up. Just hang out with me, Jimmy, and make me laugh, and then I'll go back to the office and keep trying.'

"So we stop talking about it, and we start watching television. One of those news specials is on about Robert Chambers. You remember him? The preppy murderer?"

"Yeah, yeah, the kid who 'accidentally' strangled his girlfriend during rough sex in Central Park."

"That's the one. So in the middle of it all, the kid gets caught on tape with a bunch of half-naked girls romping around, and he's twisting the head off a doll. The girls' faces are like fuzzed out to protect the guilty. It was the first time anyone did that kind of effect."

"I remember, I remember."

"So Vine starts laughing and says, 'I got it, I got it—we'll have a smoker, and his face is all digitized out, to protect the guilty.' And he's laughing, and I'm laughing. And then he stops cold and stares at me.

"'Holy shit,' he says. 'I'm trying to come up with a concept for a video wall for a huge press conference where Philip Morris is trying to tell the world not to be too quick to ban smoking everywhere—because smokers spend like a bazillion dollars on trips and in restaurants and buying cars and so on.'

"So I have no idea what he's talking about, but he's all excited. And he stands up and says, 'We'll call it "A Clear Picture of the American Smoker." The smoker's face starts out all fuzzy. And then, by the end of the video, after we bombard them with all the facts, the smoker's face will be fully visible.'

"And he runs out, just like that. Leaves his vodka on the bar. The next day he comes in at noon and tells me they won the project. Says he presented it with no visual aids—just his hands—and they loved it."

I wonder if Jimmy is just telling a story.

"That's quite a story, Jimmy. Philip Morris went on to become one of H&V's biggest clients ever."

"They did at that."

"Well, we better get going. See you tomorrow, Jimmy!"

Rach takes my arm and we head out. I feel like a million bucks, and it's not just because of the clothes.

*   *

We head down toward the West Village, stopping to get a nice bottle of cab and then a chocolate mousse hazelnut thing at a tiny little bakery.

Paul's apartment is just off Bleecker and Christopher. It's a pretty decent-sized one-bedroom on the third floor of a ten-story building. We seem to be the last to arrive, and I'm welcomed like a dear old friend.

There are about a dozen people, including Ramon and a gorgeous date, Dougie and an equally large boyfriend, and three other couples—two gay and one straight.

I decide to truly forget about Leary and H&V for an evening. It turns out to be much easier than I thought. The wine flows, the conversation flows, and an amazing dinner flows. Before I know it, we're all dancing in Paul's tiny living room and singing at the top of our lungs.

Just what the doctor ordered.

During dessert, Paul gives a special speech, during which I'm awarded an Honorary Gay Man certificate. I've never been prouder in my life.

It's after one when the party finally breaks up. After lots of hugs and kisses good-bye, Rach and I wander over toward Eighth Avenue so she can grab a cab uptown.

We're both feeling no pain, and we've got our arms around each other. I'm in a really good mood.

I don't know what comes over me, maybe I'm just caught

up in the moment, but I make a pass at her. An awkward, half-drunk, rather clumsy pass.

Rach looks at me in absolute surprise. The moment, if there was one, is gone. I've broken her golden rule. She hails a cab, I get the door for her, and she's gone.

*   *

Pitch Minus 4 Days—Sunday

I wake up the next morning with a slight hangover and a worse feeling of having screwed up with Rach. I remember a long, soul-searching subway ride last night.

I've done my best to ignore my feelings for Rachel from the instant I met her. We actually started at H&V in the same "class." Our first day was an orientation, and there were probably twenty of us. Halliday spoke, Vine spoke—it was great. We felt like we were part of the grand history of one of the best agencies in the world.

I met her during lunch—a buffet type of thing—and we immediately hit it off. We sat together for the rest of the day and did a lot of laughing. Within a few weeks, we were onto our schedule of having lunch together at least three times a week, as our schedules allowed.

She helped me understand how the creative development process worked, and I helped her understand account management. It wasn't a formal thing, but more a mutual venting process whereby we both came to understand how the other half worked.

Over the years, we've cried on each other's shoulders about lousy relationships, been the stand-in date at friends' weddings or family events when we didn't want to show up alone. We used to refer to each other as the "stunt date."

But I realize now, in my weakened state, how much I've been in love with her. But Rachel was very clear on her rules. "I don't date where I work." And she's right. H&V, like any other place of work, is a major rumor and gossip mill. It's perfectly normal; everyone does it, and everyone denies that they do it. But we've seen many an office romance end in disaster—and with one or both parties ending up leaving or getting fired.

So I've broken her golden rule, and I couldn't have done it at a worse time. The last thing I need right now is any weirdness between us.

I pull the covers over my head. I don't want to get out of

bed. I don't want to go to Jimmy's. I don't want to think about H&V or Leary or anything.

I wish I had a dog.

*   *

An hour later, I'm up, showered, shaved, dressed, and out the door. I'm drinking a cup of coffee as I head to the subway.

I don't have time to wallow. Better to get up and do. If there's a problem with Rach, then I'll hit it head-on.

*   *

I get to the war room around noon. The ever-loyal Marissa is there. Jeremy, too. No Rach.

I spend some time going over the slides that Marissa and Jeremy have created. They're solid. We'll need to add an overall look and feel, once we have one, but the content is good.

Jeremy has used a huge font to emphasize the numbers themselves. They don't need a lot of embellishing.

Marissa's slides are a beautiful collage of competitive activity that stresses the huge diversity of styles and looks that are popping up all over the place.

I tell them how great they are. I just wish I had the big idea to tie it all together.

The two of them take off to Central Park to enjoy the weather for a few hours. There's not really much more they can do until I establish an overall direction.

I'm left by myself.

Should I give Rach a call? Text her? Crap. I hate when I have to second-guess myself.

About an hour goes by. I'm jotting down some notes and playing with some ideas when suddenly the stairs up to the war room explode with footsteps, noise, clanking, and voices.

A whirlwind of activity bursts in. Rach is first, carrying her video camera and a tripod. She is followed by Marissa, Jeremy, Dougie, Ramon, Paul, and a few of the kids from the basketball game. Then there's Dave, carrying two cases of lighting equipment.

Rach blurts out, "We have no idea if this will be helpful or not, but we thought it could be really cool to tape some of the people you've met—all talking about their take on fashion and Leary and whatnot."

I'm so profoundly glad to see her that she could be telling me anything and I'd agree. But this is a good idea.

"Let's do it!"

It feels so good to have a clear mission. Everyone starts setting up, and before we know it, we've got a ministudio going. Rach is behind the camera, Marissa is making sure she's getting it captured on her Mac, Dave is adjusting lights, and Jeremy is pitching in wherever needed. Jimmy is watching from the doorway.

Once we're all set up, Ramon sits in the interviewee's chair. I'm off camera and asking the questions.

We shoot Ramon for about fifteen minutes, and it's quite fascinating. It comes out much better than I expected. He speaks with authority and insight about what's really going on when you get your hands dirty behind the scenes.

Dougie blows us away with his knowledge. He is hilarious at times, but this is balanced by his amazing eye for what matters and what doesn't. He's been doing this for over twenty years, and his expertise shines through.

Paul talks about how gay men play such a huge role in dictating tastes as advance influencers. He also surprises us when he mentions that Leary has an awful reputation as a place for gays to work, and that it has affected the company's appeal among the community. He looks right at the camera and says that Leary is missing out on both talent and sales with its attitude.

Something very different happens when we start interviewing the high school kids. It's their wonderful lack of knowledge and pretense that is so fascinating. They tell it like it is, and why they love what they love. What also comes through is how important their own look and style is to them. What they wear is who they are.

And they hold no punches when it comes to saying what they like and don't like about Leary. I'm hoping that one of them says "that Muffy and Buffy bullshit," and I'm not disappointed.

When we finish with the kids, I get another surprise. Three of the supermodels from the preview show wander in. Dougie and Ramon rush to meet them, and then the three of them stare at me, hands on hips.

Oh shit. They thought I was gay. The three of them come straight toward me, and each gives me a playful slap across the face.

Their interview is just as hard hitting as the rest. They talk about how they're treated by the different designers, and how they feel completely left out of the process by Leary. One of them blurts out, "They treat us like crap over there."

I watch the activity as we wind down. Our visitors take off a few at a time. Ramon and Dougie have assured us that they don't know what we're really doing. They were told that we're doing a research project. Whew.

Pretty soon it's back to the core gang. I notice that Rach is always too busy when I come near. The weirdness is very much alive. I decide not to push it. When everything is all packed up, she takes off with a wave and heads out with Marissa and Jeremy.

I definitely blew it. And I'm alone again.

As much as I love what we did today, I still have the huge nagging feeling that, just like Marissa and Jeremy's slides, it doesn't really mean anything without the overall concept.

My phone buzzes with a text. It's Kristina. I completely forgot.

Are you coming?

Hmmm. Sit here alone and try to come up with ideas? Or go hang out with a gorgeous model, even if she thinks I'm someone I'm not?

What the heck. I'm getting nowhere anyway.

On my way.

Five smiley faces come back at me.

She lives in the newly gentrified part of the East Village. I head out and walk toward the subway.

I get off the number 6 at Waverly and head east. I stop in a liquor store and pick up a bottle of wine. Don't want to walk in empty-handed.

I still haven't decided whether to tell her that I'm not a Bulgarian named Alexi. I figure with my luck there'll be another Bulgarian at the party, and I'll be doomed.

I find her building and ring the buzzer.

"Alexi?"

"*Da.*"

Oops, that's Russian. She buzzes me in. She's on the fourth floor. I take the elevator, get off, and find her door. I take a deep breath and knock.

She opens the door, gives me a huge smile, and envelopes me in a big hug. She smells heavenly. She is even more beautiful than I remember.

She takes my arm and we enter her small but very tasteful apartment.

"Everyone, this is Alexi."

There are two other couples. The women must also be models, and maybe the guys as well. There's Julie, Wayne, Suzette, and Kyle.

I shake the guys' hands and exchange air kisses with the gals. I'm about to take Kristina into the kitchen to explain everything when she says, "Alexi is starring in a huge new campaign for a new Bulgarian vodka, and he's going to help me get a meet with the creative director."

So that answers that question. Meet the gravy train. So Alexi it is.

They're all excited about my success.

"What's the name of the vodka?"

Good question.

"Es Republika. With K, not C. Much cool that way."

They all start bubbling with enthusiasm. The questions fly, and my struggling for the English words buys me time to make up my answers.

"Es, how you say, super premium. Best, best stuff. Super good.

"Shoots will be all over—New York, Chicago, 'ollywood. Will need extra models, yes. You have headshoots here? Very good, very good."

Of course they have their headshoots here.

As the night wears on, I'm finding it to be a powerful elixir, this feeling of being the center of attention and wielding a bit of power. It's fake, but they don't know that.

I'm starting to feel what it must be like to rise through the ranks of power of the fashion world. You must start to lose perspective as the people around you fawn and agree with you. Here I am with three stunning woman, and any one of them would probably sleep with me to get this job. Both Suzette and Julie have both slipped me their numbers when the others weren't looking.

I can only imagine what it must be like to be at the very top of the food chain like Annette or Mitchell or any of the other huge names. You must come to feel like you can do no wrong. No wonder they've lost touch.

I decide to just enjoy myself. We get drunk, we eat salad (of course), and we talk and gossip.

They could go all night, but I say I have an early meeting and must get my "beauty sleeps." They understand, but

Kristina makes it very clear that I am welcome to stay the night, with benefits. As tempted as I am, I beg off. Air kisses, air kisses, hugs, hugs, promises to speak soon, yes, I have all the headshoots, good night, good night.

So here I am again, alone and drunk and horny, heading home to my crappy apartment. And still no brainstorm.

*   *

I can't sleep. I'm tossing and turning. My mind is going a million miles a minute. I need to sleep, but it's eluding me. I keep focusing on random thoughts, such as what will happen when the bitch meets Don? What did Kristina think when she called my number and it wasn't Alexi's voice that answered? Where was the kid bending the spoon when I met Momma Oracle? The mind is a strange and mysterious thing.

Of course I finally fall asleep at 5:00 AM and then can't get up when my alarm goes off at 6:00.

*   *

Pitch Minus 3 Days—Monday

I hit H&V a bit later than usual. I get onto an empty elevator and start hitting the Close Door button.

And then who gets on but Jack Halliday himself, looking very dapper in a beautiful suit and wearing some kind of expensive cologne. He looks at me and smiles.

"So how's the big pitch coming along, sir?"

He turns to look at me. He seems surprised that I would ask so direct a question.

"Now that's the million-dollar question, isn't it?"

"More like a hundred-and-fifty-million-dollar question, sir."

He chuckles.

"I guess I'll know more later today when I see the pitch."

We get to my floor first, of course, and I start to step off. I hear him mutter something under his breath.

"Sure wish Peter was here."

I pretend not to hear, as I don't think he meant to say it out loud.

"Have a good day, sir."

"You too, young man."

*   *

I'm walking to my cube when it hits me. Vine. The person I'm supposed to talk to is Vine. That's what Momma Oracle was talking about.

I've got to talk to Vine, the man no one has been able to find. The mystery man.

I get to my cube and boot up. I've got voice mails, e-mails, and a few texts, and my cell is already vibrating.

But I don't care. I ignore them all. Finally I have a mission.

I'm racking my brain. Googling him yields nothing but a

million articles about his work and his disappearance. I plow through articles anyway. Nothing.

Who would know? Does he have family somewhere? Is he still married? Are they still together?

There are like a million Vines out there. No way to know if they're related without first names.

Who at the agency was he closest to? Most of them are gone. There's Halliday, of course, and Miriam. But she wouldn't know, and wouldn't tell me if she did.

I close my eyes and picture his office. His secretary. I remember her! A sweet old lady who was like the agency den mother. Everyone loved her. She always had candy at her desk, and she was always baking stuff and bringing it in.

Name, name, what was her name?

It doesn't come to me. Crap.

How do you go about finding someone who's disappeared? Hire a private investigator, that's how. But I've got no time and no money.

Maybe Nate could hack into something. I'll ask him.

Wait, wait, wait. Halliday's assistant. They were practically sisters. Same age, but Halliday's was much tougher. She's become very withdrawn these past few years. Protective.

Screw it. I run back to the elevators and head up to the top floor, corner office.

Name. What's her name? I'm pretty sure she has a nameplate on her desk.

*   *

I get off on 17, pass the trolls' offices, and head right to the corner office. I remember once hearing that if you walk like you belong there, people will assume that you do.

When Halliday and Vine had offices next door to each other, the place was always humming—people running in and out with stuff to show or discuss. Now it's quiet. Much too quiet.

Halliday's door is closed. Good.

And there's—nameplate please—Delores! Of course.

I realize that I've come up here so fast that I've got no plan. Sometimes no plan is a good plan. I figure I'll just tell her the truth.

She looks up at me with a questioning look. Not mean or hostile, just "what is an account exec doing up here?"

"Hello, young man. How can I help you?"

"Hi, Delores. I've met you a few times. I'm Ryan Simmons. I work on Flake-Off."

"So how can I help you, Mr. Ryan Simmons of Flake-Off? I hope you're not here to tell me I've got a dandruff problem."

Humor. She's got a sense of humor. Humor is good.

"I need your help. It's that simple."

She must see something in my eyes. She picks up her phone and hits the intercom button.

"Mr. Halliday, I'm going on a break. Be back in a few."

"Fine, Delores," comes the response.

She grabs her pocketbook.

"Let's go get a cup of coffee, Mr. Ryan Simmons."

I figure we're going to just go to the pantry, but we head toward the elevator, and before I know it, we're at a Starbucks around the corner. Delores orders a black Grande. I go for a Venti Latte.

"So how can I help you?"

"How did you know that I wanted to get out of the building?"

"Call it intuition."

"I need to find Mr. Vine. I've got to talk to him."

She laughs.

"What is this, another bet among the AEs to see who can find him?"

"No, ma'am. I remember that though. I lost a lot of money on that one."

"I have no idea where he is. I don't even know if he's alive. Why do you want to see him?"

"I'm trying to save this place."

This is not what she was expecting. She looks at me. I'm going to have to give if I'm going to get anything from this savvy old bird.

"You miss him, don't you?"

Again, not what she was expecting. She looks off for a minute, and I don't interrupt her.

"It was a very different time, young man. I loved it here when Peter was around. Jack loved it when Peter was around. They were the most dynamic duo you ever saw. They wooed clients like you wouldn't believe. Peter with his ideas, and Jack with his charm. Watching them work together was like watching Matthew Broderick and Nathan Lane on Broadway together.

"It was a different business back then. It was sexy and glamorous. And it was about relationships, not return on investment. And the best of the best wanted to work here.

"Now it's all just the numbers. The good Duke wouldn't care if we were selling chain saws and tractors. He just cares about margins and utilization. Jack hates it now. He so wants to either buy the company back or get out. But it's still his name on the door.

"And there was laughter. So much laughter up there on 17. When Peter and Jack started telling stories, oh my gosh."

"I remember Mr. Vine. He was why I came here. I was in a few meetings with him. He was just amazing to watch."

Silence for a bit. Then I break in.

"What really happened?"

"The stories you've heard are pretty much true. The Four Seasons and the crew from G&P."

"I mean afterward. Why did they force him out?"

"Money, Mr. Simmons. Money. Duke Owen was already spending the billings from those new G&P brands. IMH was burning through cash gobbling up agencies all over the world. A few major deals fell through because of 'the incident.'

"And Duke Owen never really understood what an agency was. That it has a creative soul. Peter was that soul. And Owen killed it."

"Did he have a choice?"

"Of course he had a choice. What nobody knows is that the G&P folks felt horrible about the whole thing. They understood that it was mental illness. Their CEO and Jack were on the phone the whole week afterward. They actually wanted to keep the business here. They loved Peter and his work.

"But Duke Owen used it as the excuse he needed to get rid of Peter. There was a clause in his contract that allowed IMH to get rid of him for peanuts if he violated their standards clause."

"Like a morals clause for athletes?"

"Just like that."

"So not only did Peter get fired in disgrace, he also got less money than he could have."

"That's right, Ryan. But he still did okay on the initial sale."

We both sip our coffee for a minute or so.

"I've never told anyone this. I don't know why I told you."

"Why did you tell me?"

"Because I believe what you said, that you're trying to save the place."

"So where's Vine?"

"I really don't know."

"Someone must. Doesn't Jack?"

"He doesn't. He's tried to find him as well. Peter doesn't

want to see Jack. Or talk to him. I think he blames him to some degree."

"And you were in the middle of it?"

"That was the worst part. Peter wasn't rational. I'd seen times when he went off his medications. He hated them. They made him tired, and he didn't get to feel the highs of his mania. But this was much worse. He was lashing out at everyone and had to be hospitalized."

"What happened to his secretary? I can't remember her name."

"You didn't remember mine either. I saw you glance at my nameplate."

"Busted."

She laughs.

"Her name was Esther, and she was what you kids would call my BFF. We worked together for almost thirty years. We were hired on the same day—Jack and Peter were arguing over which one of us would work for whom. They thought we couldn't hear them through the wall. We started out in a hole-in-the-wall little office. There were weeks at a time that they couldn't pay us, but we all hung in there, and then things just took off. And Jack and Peter took very good care of us."

"Where's Esther now?"

"I don't think I can tell you that. She's fanatical about her privacy."

"Do you still keep in touch?"

"We do, but it hasn't been the same. We used to do everything together. Then she was just gone. The Duke didn't think it would be good to have her around reminding everyone of Peter, so he basically made her a deal to leave immediately. She was going to stay just to piss him off—she wasn't afraid of anybody, despite her sweet image. But it would have been financial suicide for her to stay. That bastard."

"Do you think she'd talk to me?"

"No."

"That sounds pretty black and white."

"She was so hurt that she vowed never to have anything to do with H&V. When we do talk, she won't let me tell her anything. So our relationship has gotten a bit strained over the past few years."

"Would you let me try? Would you give me her phone number?"

"That wouldn't help you. She doesn't answer her phone, and she won't call you back."

"I'll go visit her. Can you give me her address? Is she still in this area?"

"I'll give you her address. I don't know why. Call it intuition again. You remind me of a young Jack."

"That means a lot to me."

"She lives in Brooklyn. Her husband passed away last year, so she keeps to herself."

She writes it down for me.

"I'll go right now."

"Good luck, Mr. Ryan Simmons."

We stand.

"Thank you, Delores. Do you think she knows where he is?"

"I don't know. But if anyone does, she does."

*   *

We leave the Starbucks and head our separate ways. I'm still ignoring my cell, but I glance at the caller ID as it vibrates again. It's Rach. I answer it.

"Hey, Rach."

"Ry, I've got great news. I think. I'm in the room. Drew wants me in the pitch. We're presenting this afternoon to Jack, and I'm in the room."

"That is great. I'm surprised, but that's great."

"I'm not presenting anything, but I think they want me

there for visual balance. I'm the only woman. Drew actually told me to dress 'funky' for the actual pitch."

"Now it makes sense. He wants you there as eye candy for Mitchell. And to make us look cool."

"I'd like to think that it's because of my brain, but I think you're right."

"Who else is in?"

"Drew, Chas, Jack, me, and of course a tech guy to run things."

"No Miriam? No interactive people?"

"Nope."

"Is The Duke coming in?"

"We think so, but we're not 100 percent sure. But I think he is."

"He probably will. He's probably already spending the fees."

"Where are you, by the way?"

"I'm on a bit of a mission. Let's see if I succeed or fail."

"Okay. I won't bug you."

"Rach, I'm—"

"I know. Don't sweat it, Ry. Good luck with whatever you're doing."

"Thanks, Rach. Let me know how it goes with Jack."

"Will do. Bye."

"Bye."

Relief courses through me. Weirdness seems to be gone. I head down into the subway to check the map and figure out how to get to Park Slope.

*　　　*

I love the outer boroughs, but I also hate them. It's very easy to get lost. I'm wandering down a street in a nice enough neighborhood—one of those streets with the three-story houselike things that have the long front stairs. I've been lost for the last half hour, but now I'm getting close. And there it is, 1024 Wilmot Street. I take a deep breath, walk up the stairs, and ring the bell.

I hear noise and then the door opens. And there's Esther, just like I remember her. Bright, friendly eyes and just an overall warmth. I swear I can smell something baking.

She opens the door but does not invite me in, but I see a flicker of recognition in her eyes.

"I remember you. You're from H&V. What do you want? Why have you come all the way out here?

"Hi, Esther. I'm Ryan Simmons. I just spent the last hour with Delores, and here I am."

"I'm doing my best to forget about H&V."

"I don't blame you, but I need your help. It's that simple."

"I'm sorry, young man, but I really can't help you."

She starts to close the door.

"Are those oatmeal cookies? I remember your oatmeal cookies. They were my favorite."

"That's not going to work. But I do appreciate it."

"They were Peter's favorite, too."

"Now how would you know that?"

"Because he ate like ten of them during a meeting once. We were all dying to try them, and we watched them disappear one by one. None of us dared to take one."

The door still isn't open, but it's not closed either.

"Actually, his favorite was peanut butter. But oatmeal ran a close second."

"I remember the chocolate chip, but not the peanut butter."

"Tell me what you want to know. Straight up. No nonsense."

"I need to get in touch with Peter. I need his help."

She gives me a look that penetrates me to my core.

"I don't know where he is. I'm sorry."

This time the door does close. So much for no plan is a good plan. But she knows. I could see it in her eyes. But what can I do?

I'm about to knock again but think better of it. I don't want to push her. She's already been too hurt. Maybe I was wrong and this was a stupid idea.

I head down the stairs. My phone is going nuts, but I really don't care.

I remember a small park a few blocks away. I walk over and sit on a bench. It's a tiny bit chilly, but the sun is shining and it feels good.

It's just about two o'clock. The presentation to Jack must be starting.

I decide I better reconnect. I call my voice mail at the office first. One message from the bitch—she's really pissed off that I haven't followed-up on the layouts. If she only knew. Another from Bruce asking me to stop by.

Texts next. Not one, not two, but three texts from Kristina asking if I've shown her headshoots—smiley smiley—to the creative director yet?

Another from Marissa checking in. Am I coming by soon? Do I have an idea yet?

Next up, e-mail. Crap. Forty-eight new messages. I quickly get rid of ten spams and five newsletters. Two messages from Bruce—one telling me to stop by, another that is a forward from Chas confirming that there wasn't a fight. Great. Now I can bury his ass if I want to. Bruce's e-mail ends with a ???

Three from the bitch of increasing intensity demanding the layouts. She has a meeting at 5:00 with her boss to show them. I had e-mailed Chas over the weekend asking for a time frame on the layouts. I scroll through my messages looking for his response.

And there it is. From Chas to the team.

Hey, all.

As you know, the shoot last Friday did not go smoothly. Unfortunately, our representative from the account team did not show up, and therefore the photographer refused to proceed, as she did not have confidence that the shoot would be paid for. This forced us to cancel the shoot.

We are now in the position of having to reschedule the shoot for this Wednesday. Given this time frame, we anticipate having layouts to the client by the following Monday.

Please let me know if you have any questions or comments.

Chas

What a piece of work. Time to make some stuff happen. I call Marissa.

"Hi, Ry."

"Hey, Marissa. I need a huge favor. I need you to do your magic. You ready to write?"

"Go ahead."

"Login to my Webmail account—password is max123, after my first dog. Check my Sent folder for an e-mail to the bitch last Thursday with a shot attached. Check in my Flake-Off Copy folder for an e-mail with the most-recent version of the copy.

"Then whip out two layouts—you know what she likes— and get them off to her. She needs them by 4:30. You'll see an e-mail from her in my Inbox. Respond to it and tell her she'll have them in time.

"You got all that? Can you do it?"

"I'm on it. Consider it done."

"You so totally rock. I'm working on something and will get back to you. Thanks!"

I hang up.

I go back to Chas's e-mail and respond to the team.

> All—
>
>   Chas's response below is filled with so many inaccuracies that I can't address them all, as I'm remote and typing with my thumbs. The unapproved shoot of last week was a total mess because Chas had a major fight with his girlfriend, the photographer, and they both stormed out. It had nothing to do with the fact that I was not present.
>
>   The rescheduled shoot for Wednesday is unapproved and completely unnecessary. The client has emphatically requested the layouts by 5:00 PM today. She will be very disappointed if she doesn't receive them. This could have easily been accomplished had we proceeded with the shots she approved last week.
>
> Ryan

I decide to cc the trolls. I hit Send. Oh boy. What a complete waste of time.

I start cruising through the rest of my e-mails when I smell what can only be fresh-baked oatmeal cookies. I look up and there's Esther, holding a plate of cookies and a thermos. She sits next to me. I take a cookie, and she pours me a cup of coffee. I take a bite and smile. We sit together for a few minutes enjoying the sun. I figure she'll start talking when she's ready.

"Even now, after everything that's happened, I can't hate

H&V. I do hate Duke Owen Pollard, but H&V was my home for thirty years. Delores and I were there from practically day one.

"You wouldn't believe the times we had. The holiday parties. The celebrations when we had a big win. We went through some tough times, too, but we were like a family. We did what we had to. There were months at a time that Jack and Peter didn't take a paycheck. The employees always came first."

She stares off.

"So why do you need to speak with Peter?"

"Because Drew is about to destroy the place. They're going to blow the last chance we have for a major win."

"Don't mention that man. That man is evil. House of Leary, right?"

She is keeping up.

"Yup. My friend is on the pitch team. She showed me the campaigns. They're awful."

"What's her name?"

"Rachel. Rachel Weiss."

"I remember her. Smart girl. Pretty. In a different kind of way."

"Yes, that's Rach."

"So what are you doing about it? What's the plan?"

I make a split-second decision.

"We have a crazy crew of renegades coming up with an alternate pitch. We have a war room over at Ar."

"How is Jimmy? I miss him."

"I think he's having a blast helping us."

"I'm sure he is. Bit of a rebel, that one."

"We're doing our homework, but we're not there yet. My gut is just telling me to talk to Peter."

"What does Jack think?"

"He's actually seeing the concepts right now. But he doesn't stand up to Drew."

"Jack without Peter is like Laurel without Hardy."

I haven't had lunch. I take another cookie.

"So how are you going to get into the pitch?"

"No clue. I'm operating without a total plan here, Esther. But how we get in is irrelevant at this point if we don't have anything to present."

"This is true."

"You said you've done your homework. What have you done?"

I tell her everything. I have her in stitches when I describe my makeover by Ramon, Dougie's dance, and how Kristina still thinks I'm Alexi. I hold nothing back. The cookies are gone by the time I'm done.

"You've done a lot in one week. And that was quite ballsy of you to go over to Drew at the fashion show."

"There's so much juggling around in my head right now. I know something's there. But I can't get to it."

I finish the last of the coffee. The time has come.

"Is he okay?"

"That's not really a yes-or-no answer, I'm afraid. How much do you really know about mental illness? I mean true mental illness. Not crazy girlfriends or strange uncles."

"Some, but not a ton. I've had some friends who've had pretty serious issues. And one of my aunts has always been pretty depressed."

"Peter was diagnosed as a true manic-depressive. I didn't really know what that meant for many years, but I certainly remember his highs and lows. I thought that just was who he was. I figured that came with his creativity.

"But one afternoon I came into his office, and he was literally hiding under his desk. He wouldn't move. He was shaking and holding his knees, and he was scared to death. At first I thought he was joking around, but he wasn't.

"Jack was wonderful with him. He understood. He could

always calm Peter down. We'd close the door and stay with him until he came back to us.

"And the highs. It's true what they say, that being with a manic-depressive when they're cycling high is more fun than a barrel of monkeys. Peter could do anything when he was in his manic phases. He was truly brilliant, and he was so much fun. We'd go out to a club with a group from the agency, and Peter would hold court for hours, telling stories and buying drinks. It was so much fun!

"Years later, when he was actually diagnosed, it was a constant battle for me and Jack and Peter's wife, Ann, to keep him on his medication. I really don't know what was worse, dealing with the highs and the lows or seeing how miserable the medicine made him.

"But Peter always came through when a pitch was on the line or a client needed something breakthrough. What a mind!

"He was crushed when Duke Owen forced him out. His whole life was H&V. He was absolutely lost."

She is looking off, and her eyes are moist.

"Ann asked me to help. We were like sisters, so I spent time up at their home in Rye sometimes. Then it got so bad that we had to put him in a hospital for a few months.

"When he got out, they sold the home in Rye and moved up to the Berkshires. Peter and Ann loved it up there—they'd vacation there whenever they could. They bought a small house on a lake. I've been there. It's lovely.

"When was the last time you saw him?"

"A few months ago, during the holidays. It's so beautiful up there in the winter."

"The Berkshires aren't that far. I could drive there in a few hours."

"You're a very determined young man."

"I'm not letting H&V go down without a fight. Too many people's jobs are on the line."

My phone rings. Caller ID says its Rach. I show the phone to Esther, and she nods for me to take it.

"Hey, Rach. How'd it go?"

"It was weird. That's all I can say. Jack didn't seem to be that enthusiastic, but Drew told him it was perfect, it was just what they wanted, blah, blah, blah. They say they want something different, but they really don't. Jack didn't really know what to do, so the meeting ended and we all left. Drew really didn't care what Jack thought anyway; he viewed it as a total rubber stamp. Where are you, by the way?"

"I'm sitting on a park bench out in Park Slope. I just had about eight of Esther's oatmeal-raisin cookies."

"Esther? Peter's Esther?"

"She's sitting right next to me."

"Oh, please tell her I say hello—and that we all miss her."

I tell Esther, and she beams. Then Rachel gasps.

"You're trying to find Peter! Oh my God, you're trying to find the man who can't be found!"

I look at Esther. She nods.

"I gotta run, Rach. I'm leaving for the Berkshires in an hour."

*   *

Once Esther made up her mind, she became a whirlwind of helping me get going. She even insists that I take her car—a beautifully maintained 1967 Dodge Charger that belonged to her husband. Oh man. My day just got a bit better. Better than a crappy rental.

She also packs me enough food for at least three weeks (and sneaks in another container of cookies). She's also given me directions, including a hand-drawn map of the last few miles, explaining that it's really hard to find.

Her home isn't far from mine, so I zip home and grab a

few things—I assume I won't be coming back until tomorrow. It should take about three hours to get there. I'm officially on my way around four o'clock.

The Berkshires is a beautiful mountain range in the western part of Massachusetts and Connecticut. The region is beautiful and mostly rural, but it's also filled with great restaurants and rich in culture, including music, theater, and museums. Not to mention, there are antiques galore.

It's a beautiful day, and I'm on the road in a badass car, heading toward one of the nicest areas in New England. I've got my sunglasses on and the music blaring. I should be enjoying this. I am enjoying this. Except that I'm not enjoying this. What the hell am I doing?

I know that I shouldn't drive and read e-mail at the same time. I'm glancing back and forth between the road and my phone.

I see the e-mail sent by Marissa to the bitch, and the bitch's reply—they look good and she's showing them to her boss.

Whew.

I call Bruce and get his voice mail. I leave a message telling him I'm taking care of everything remotely and not to worry. I forward him the e-mail from the bitch; he'll be confused as hell, but I'll explain later. I also tell him I have to take care of something personal but am available by cell and e-mail.

I see a reply from Chas. I pull over to read it.

> All—
>
> I refuse to address Ryan's ludicrous accusations by e-mail. I reiterate that this is a creative agency, and creative decides when materials are released to the client and when they are not.
>
> The shoot for Wednesday is on, and there will be a meeting on Tuesday between

account and creative to resolve these issues
once and for all.

Chas

Good. Maybe we can end this lunacy. I e-mail back that I
can hardly wait for the meeting.

I pull back on and hit the Grand Central Parkway. Once
I'm over the Triboro Bridge, I'll be heading north and out of
here.

I call Marissa.

"Hey, Ry."

"Marissa, thank you so much for getting that done. You
are amazing."

"Won't you get in trouble?"

"Probably. You know how doing the right thing for the
client is always the wrong move."

"Where are you, anyway?"

"I'm just going over the Triboro Bridge. I'm in an
immaculate 1967 Dodge Charger, I've got my shades on, and
as soon as I get off the phone, I'll turn the music back up. And
I've got a full tin of Esther's oatmeal cookies sitting on the seat
next to me."

"Esther? Our Esther? Peter's Esther?"

"The very one. It's her car."

"Ryan, what the hell are you doing?"

"I'm heading up to the Berkshires."

She finally gets it.

"You found Peter! You're going to talk to Peter. Oh my
God, that is so cool!"

"I have no idea if he'll even see me. But I'm listening to
my gut."

"What can I do in the meantime?"

"It would be great if you could start editing the stuff
we shot yesterday. Start by stringing together clips of where

they're all saying negative things about Leary. That's the only thought I have now. Let's talk later after you've been through it all; maybe we'll come up with more ideas."

"On it, Ry. And good luck!"

"Thanks."

I make another call.

"Santa Claus, this is Easter Bunny. How's Operation Mistletoe coming along?"

"As planned. Mr. Don is not so much the Juan anymore. He's very confused, but he just e-mailed the female dog, and he was as sweet and contrite as can be."

"You are truly the master, and I bow to you. By the way, what did you think of the pitch? You were in there, right?"

"Of course I was. I've been in every pitch this company has made for the last fifteen years. And I can tell you with absolute certainty that it was the worst piece of shit I've ever seen. But what do I know? I'm just the hired help."

"Yeah, Rach said the same thing. What did Jack think?"

"He didn't like it. But there's really nothing he can do about it. He's lost without Peter."

There it is again.

"Yeah, you're right."

"Where are you, anyway?"

"I'm in a vintage 1967 Dodge Charger heading north to a beautiful cabin on a lake in the Berkshires."

"Yeah right."

"Later, Nate."

"Bye."

If he only knew.

*   *

The next few hours turn out to be wonderful. It's hard to stay uptight as the miles roll by, the city gets farther and farther away, and the scenery gets more and more beautiful.

My cell keeps going off, but I ignore it. Time to just get off the grid.

I've been on the Taconic State Parkway for about an hour and am about to get off and use local routes.

It's about six o'clock. I've got about an hour to go, and it's starting to get dark. My destination is Stockbridge, Massachusetts. It's supposed to be a great town, filled with history and home to a museum dedicated to Norman Rockwell, its most famous resident.

I wind my way north and, despite myself, find that I'm relaxing more and more. The fresh air, the scenery—I feel myself slowing down.

About forty-five minutes later, I pull into Stockbridge. It's a picture-perfect postcard of a New England town. A few main streets, the museum, some charming-looking inns and restaurants.

Thank God for Esther's directions: signs are rare once you get out of town. She has me looking for things like "the yellow house with the gazebo" and "a mailbox that has a big rooster on it."

The sun is down by now, and I almost miss a few landmarks. But before I know it, I'm on a tiny dirt driveway heading toward a beautiful cabin on a stunning lakefront. The name on the mailbox says Root. They must have changed their name.

Suddenly I'm nervous. I cut the lights. What the hell am I doing? These people don't know me. I've met Peter like three times, in big groups. I've never met his wife. And here I am invading their very carefully guarded privacy in the middle of nowhere.

I'm agonizing about what to do when the door opens and both of them step out onto the little front porch. They obviously recognize the car, so they're not concerned. Maybe Esther called to warn them. But she said she wouldn't—we didn't want to give them a chance to say no.

I get out of the car, and then they are surprised. I'm obviously not Esther. I say the first thing that comes to mind.

"I've got oatmeal-raisin cookies for you. They're not peanut butter, which I know are your favorite, but they came out of the oven a few hours ago."

I hold up the tin.

Peter smiles broadly and comes over. Ann looks a bit wary. Peter takes the tin, opens it, takes a cookie, bites into it, and smiles.

"I know your face. I can't remember your name."

"Ryan. Ryan Simmons."

"Well, I'm going to assume that you didn't tie up Esther and steal her car, so then she must have a good reason for telling you how to get here."

"I don't mean to invade your privacy, sir, but I need your help."

"Well, you call me sir one more time and you'll be back on the highway and I'll have all the cookies. Call me Peter. C'mon in. We were just about to have dinner. Hope you like lamb. Ann, this is Ryan Simmons."

She still looks a bit wary, but she's softening.

Peter looks a bit older than I remember. He's a very good-looking man, a bit above average in height and still in good shape. His hair is longer and grayer, and his hairline is receding, but the overall effect is pleasant. Ann is quite lovely. She must have been a real looker in her day. She exudes a true warmth, and there is a sparkle of energy and intelligence in her eyes. It is also obvious how much these two love each other.

We go inside, and I actually catch my breath. What a great place; it's everything you'd expect in a country cabin. An amazing deck overlooking a pristine lake. A full country kitchen. A cozy living room with a fireplace. A full computer workstation in one corner. The overall feel is rustic but modern.

Ann sets another place at the table, and Peter pours me

a glass of cabernet. Whatever they're having, it smells great. Ann places several platters on the table as Peter serves up some salad.

We all sit. I toast to their beautiful place. The wine is excellent. I can tell that, despite the intrusion, they're both glad to have an unexpected guest, just to mix things up.

We thankfully spend the meal talking very comfortably about the Berkshires and how they rebuilt the cabin and how much their lives have changed. They ask me a lot about myself—where I live, why I don't have a girlfriend, even where I'm from and who my parents are.

The wine is taking effect with a nice buzz. We finish the meal and clean up, and Peter starts a fire. We settle around the fireplace with the last of the wine and the tin of cookies.

"So how is it that you think I can help you?"

I tell my tale for the third time today, but this time in complete detail. Peter and Ann are a wonderful audience. We're rolling with laughter throughout. Peter especially gets a kick out of the whole Momma Oracle thing and insists that he has to meet her and try her pie.

He seems truly sad that Jack can't do anything about the pitch.

"The reason why Jack and I worked so well together was that he was a master account guy and I was the creative. We knew our roles, and we worked seamlessly together. I always knew that I sucked at what he did, and he knew that he sucked at what I did. It's why we always got along so well. We needed each other, and we respected each other."

"He seems lost and unhappy right now."

"I'm sure he is."

We all stare at the fire for a bit.

"I'm going to tell you something, Ryan. Something I haven't told anyone except Ann here. Everyone at the agency, the clients, even the press figured that I was such a great creative because I was half-mad, that somehow my mental illness is what opened my mind to thinking differently and out of the box. And I did nothing to change that impression. I didn't push it, but I also did nothing to stop it. It was good for business.

"But it's bullshit. My illness had absolutely nothing to do with my success or my ability to come up with ideas. Well, maybe a little. But more than anything it got in my way. It slowed me down. It scared me. It was my own demons tearing me apart. Nothing sexy or glamorous or creative about it.

"What really did work was hard work. More work than you can imagine. Like what you're doing. I'd leave for hours, and everyone thought I was probably walking in the park muttering to myself. What I was doing was fieldwork. Depending on the client, I'd spend hours in drugstores or supermarkets or fast-food joints watching what people did, listening to them. I'd talk to store managers and sales clerks. I'd read every magazine article I could find. I'd compare products. I'd buy them and take them home and try them, cook them, tear them apart. If the client was a bank, I'd go into ten banks and pretend I needed a loan.

"And the other secret weapon I had was Miriam. Miriam is the smartest person at H&V, no question. We'd spend hours together poring over whatever research we could get our hands on. Ann here used to think we were having an affair."

"I did not."

"And sooner or later we'd find something. Some small nugget that popped out at us. And that nugget would click off something in my mind that would open the door to an idea."

I'm nodding.

"The one thing we haven't been able to get our hands on is the research. Leary sent over a ton of stuff, going back years, but they sent one copy, nothing electronic, and they want it all back if H&V loses. It's locked up in Miriam's office.

"Has Drew looked at it?"

"Kinda sorta. He had Miriam write a summary of it, and

I'm sure he read it, but from what I hear, he certainly didn't go through most of it himself."

"That's why his pitch sucks. You've got to get your hands on that research."

"I don't have much of a relationship with Miriam. She'd never let me see it."

"Well, now don't you worry about that, Mr. Ryan Simmons. I believe that you and I are going on a road trip."

*   *

Pitch Minus 2 Days—Tuesday

So now it's Tuesday morning, and we're on the road, with cups of coffee and a box of donuts and the windows open to the spring air.

Ann is in the back. She insisted that she come along to watch out for Peter, but I think she was as up for an adventure as Peter was.

I'm in a bit of a fog. After we finished talking last night at the cabin, Peter insisted that we go downtown to one of the local watering holes. It wasn't crowded on a Tuesday night, but there were enough people to fill a round table, where Peter commenced to hold court, just as Esther described.

He told stories and bought drinks. He had these farmers and yokels laughing their heads off, everyone telling jokes, doing imitations, and singing songs. It was truly a sight to behold. We finally all said good night around two o'clock, when the owner reluctantly kicked us out—he was having as good a time as the rest of us.

Now Peter's sitting in the front seat, sunglasses in place, hair flying all over the place, with a cup of coffee in one hand and a dutch apple donut in the other. He's grinning from ear to ear.

*   *

We make it back to the city in very good time—it's the middle of the day in the middle of the week, so there's not much traffic.

It's about two in the afternoon when we cross into Manhattan, and a half hour later we park in a garage near the office. Peter puts on a Yankees baseball cap and pulls it way down over his eyes. He knew a million people and doesn't want to take a chance on being recognized somewhere. He laughs and says that anyone who knows him knows that he's a Mets fan.

I head toward the office, and Peter says he's going shopping with Ann and will meet me at Ar around six.

My stomach tightens as I put my access card into the turnstile and head toward the elevators. I get off on my floor, go to my cube, and boot up.

Chas's meeting is scheduled for 4:00. I start blowing through other stuff – voice mail, e-mail, texts, everything.

The bitch has e-mailed to say the layouts were well received by her boss, and asks when we can move forward with final art. Marissa, I love you. I print this one out.

Bruce has asked that I stop by before the meeting.

The trolls have asked for a full budget analysis for the Flake-Off account.

The rest are not priority.

I have fifteen voice mail messages.

The bitch repeating the same thing as her e-mail.

Nate asking me to call him.

Bruce asking me to stop by.

The trolls, separate messages, repeating their e-mail request but with some urgency.

Drew's secretary confirming the meeting in his conference room at four.

Again, the rest are not priority.

Text from Marissa—the edits on the first part are done. They're very impactful. She's playing around with some other ideas.

Three texts from Kristina, begging me to contact her.

I jump on the phone and call Nate.

"Scooby, it's Shaggy."

"Yo."

"Update?"

"Things are progressing like clockwork. She's now playing hard to get, but they're going to talk tonight by phone."

"Amazing."

I click off and call Marissa. I tell her I'll be there at six and to keep up the good work.

I head to Bruce's office. For the first time since I've known him, he actually looks glad to see me.

"Boy, am I glad to see you."

"Sorry about being AWOL. Had to take care of some stuff."

"That's okay. Listen, this meeting coming up—word is that they're really after you."

"I know. It's okay."

"What do you mean, 'it's okay'?"

"Two things. Number one—"

I show him the e-mail approval from the bitch.

"How did you do this?"

"I've kept in touch with Marissa, and she did the layouts in like an hour and a half. No big deal. I had her do it because it was what the client needed. Not what Chas needed. And she did it as a favor."

"I get it, and as far as I'm concerned, it's great. But they'll use this against you."

"Yeah, I figured that. We'll just have to see what happens."

"You said two things."

I take out my phone and go into my media player.

"You know how Chas insisted that there wasn't a fight? And he's done it twice now, in writing."

"Yeah."

I click on the video that Dave sent. Bruce watches. Within about ten seconds he's laughing out loud. By the end, when she calls him a wuss, he's doubled over cracking up.

"Ry, this is Academy Award stuff."

"Yeah, I know."

Bruce glances at his watch.

"Oh shit. We have to go."

"Bruce, listen. You have to trust me on this. I may not use

this in the meeting today. It may happen that you're going to be absolutely dying for me to show it, begging me, and I may not. I can't explain it right now, but trust me that things will come out okay in the end."

"I never thought I'd say this, Ryan, but I trust you. Let's go."

We head to the elevators.

*   *

Bruce and I enter Drew's conference room right at 4:00. The trolls enter at 4:04. Drew and Chas, of course, don't enter until 4:10.

I don't know what possesses me, but before they even sit down, I go right on the offensive, just like last time. I stand up and toss the e-mail from the bitch across the table to them and give a copy to each of the trolls.

"I'd like to know why you guys are wasting all of our time on a project that has already been approved by the client! I'd like to know why you've scheduled yet a third unbudgeted shoot when the original shots have already been approved by the client. What the hell is going on here, Chas?"

I stay standing and glaring at him. Drew and Chas are still reading the e-mail. They're confused. The trolls have finished reading, and they're watching with just a twinge of amusement. This is an even better show than they were expecting.

Drew looks up at me slowly, with a smile as cold as ice.

"I'd like to know how the client got layouts from you when no one on our creative staff created or approved them."

"I'm sure you would. But before I answer that, I'd like to know why your creative staff refuses to deliver on time. The client made it very clear on numerous occasions that she needed layouts yesterday at 5:00 PM to show her management. Your team failed to deliver, so as the account person, I did what I had to do to get the job done for the client. Who is very happy, by the way."

Drew and Chas are taken aback by my attack. The trolls watch. Bruce is just staring. Then Drew hits back, as I knew he would.

"Listen, you little piece of dog shit, you don't make creative decisions at this agency. I don't care what happened. You do not have the authority to send creative to any client without the approval of your creative director.

"And one more thing. Don't you ever accuse one of my people of lying, and especially don't do it in writing, and especially don't copy these two. Especially when you have no proof of your accusations whatsoever."

My hand is involuntarily reaching for my cell phone. Bruce is looking at me with pleading eyes. As much as I want to do it, I have decided that Momma Oracle is the one I trust. This is just a battle, not the war.

I don't say anything. My hand is actually shaking, but I stay quiet. But I don't back down physically. I'm staring at both of them, and I'm smiling.

Drew stands. Chas stands right after him.

"This isn't over, Simmons. Consider yourself a dead man walking. I'm going to do everything in my power to get you fired. And I have a lot of power."

Bruce stands.

"Drew, rest assured that I will do everything in my power to make sure that that does not happen."

We leave. The trolls almost look like they're going to burst into applause. They haven't seen a show like this in years.

*   *

Bruce and I both keep our heads high as we head to the elevators. As soon as we get on and the door closes, we both exhale loudly.

A million conflicting emotions hit at the same time. We're ecstatic that we stood up to them. We're scared to death that we'll both end up fired. We're pumped up on adrenaline.

"Ryan, no matter what happens, I will remember this day for the rest of my life."

"Me too."

We get off and head to his office.

"Listen, Bruce, I can't tell you how much I appreciate what you just did. I'll never forget it. But don't get yourself fired over me. You've got a house and a wife and kids—you've got to protect them."

"You're right, Ryan. And I will protect them. But I've been taking crap from that asshole ever since he walked in the door of this agency. And it's about goddamn time that I grew some balls."

I laugh out loud. And then we're both laughing. It feels good.

"I've got to run."

"I know you're up to something, Ryan. I hope whatever it is, it's good."

"Thanks, Bruce."

It's twenty to six. I'm gone.

*   *

Fifteen minutes later I'm going through the door at Ar.

"Hey, Jimmy."

"Hey, Ryan. Been quiet around here without you."

"Well, that's about to change. I've got a surprise coming in about two minutes. Who's upstairs?"

"The gang. Rach, Marissa, Jeremy. Dave has kinda unofficially joined as well."

"The more the merrier."

"Where you been the last few days?"

"You'll see in a few minutes."

I sit at the bar. I'm about to say something when Peter and Ann walk through the door. Peter slowly takes off the Yankees cap, and Jimmy drops the glass he is washing and yells out loud. He leaps over the bar and envelopes Peter in a huge bear hug.

"Peter!"

"Jimmy!"

This is a reunion of true friends. Ann and Jimmy hug as well. I break in.

"C'mon, Peter, check out our war room."

We all go upstairs. Another scream follows when he walks through the door. Rach and Marissa jump up and run over to him, and Dave and Jeremy come over and shake his hand. Peter looks around. He seems pleased.

"This is great, everyone. Now Ryan and I have a little errand to run, and then we'll be right back, with another surprise."

He winks at me and we take off.

*   *

He puts the baseball cap back on as we head toward H&V. We go around the side to the freight elevator. Robbie knows me and lets us in, but he only started last year, so he doesn't know Peter.

We get off on 14 and sneak around to Miriam's office. We slip in and close the door behind us.

Miriam has been waiting for us, and she leaps up and hugs Peter.

"I can't believe it. It's really you!"

I can only hope I'll have friends like this when I get older.

"Hello, Miriam. It is so good to see you."

I've learned that with Peter, I have to play the nudge.

"I hate to rush things, but we've got to get out of here."

"Of course, of course. I've got everything ready to go. It's all right here."

There are at least five big boxes filled with binders. I can't believe how many there are. We all grab one and head to the freight elevator. I run back twice for the last two boxes.

Robbie takes us down. I grab a cab, and we pile in with the boxes and drive the few blocks to Jimmy's. We tip the cabbie nicely for his trouble.

We carry all the boxes up to the war room. Everyone jumps up, and we start laying the binders out on tables.

Peter and Miriam take off their jackets, and Peter holds up his hands.

"Listen up, everyone. Somewhere in these binders is the answer. I have no idea what we're looking for, but I know that it's in here somewhere."

With these few words, we are all rapt. Miriam steps forward.

"I've been through all of this in a top level way, but I stopped last week when it became clear that Drew didn't care anyway.

"That pile over there is the most recent. There are a ton of focus group results on that side, and three quantitative studies on that side.

"That table over there is filled with focus groups on the individual Leary brands. Over there are long-term attitude, awareness, and usage studies going back five years.

"The binders on that table are filled with press releases and articles going back at least ten years.

"And finally, over there, are trend reports from independent industry analysts going back at least five years.

"And here are copies of the summary I gave to Drew last week."

We dive in and get to work.

Jeremy hits the analyst reports, and Marissa, the individual brands.

Rach heads for the recent focus groups, and Dave, for the recent quantitative.

Peter and Miriam hit the AAUs.

And I dig into the press releases and articles.

And, of course, Jimmy arrives with sandwiches, fries, and beers for all.

*   *

Pitch Minus 1 Day—Wednesday

It becomes an all-nighter for some of us. It's about nine o'clock the next morning. Wednesday morning. This is our last day before the big day.

We made Rach leave at midnight—she had to be at work on time to continue prep for the pitch. Marissa and Jeremy stayed until two. We made them leave by telling them that we needed them strong for what was already today.

Jimmy closed up downstairs as usual, came back up for an hour, and then slept on the couch in his office. I don't think it was the first time.

Ann took off around three o'clock and went and booked a hotel room two blocks away. She still seemed nervous about leaving Peter alone, but her comfort level increased the more time she spent with us. And she knew that Jimmy and Miriam were here in case anything happened. "Adult supervision" I think is what she said.

Miriam stayed with us all night. I think she's so glad to see Peter that her energy level is higher than it's been in years. She made it to about seven, just when Jimmy got up to make us breakfast, and took his warm spot on his couch.

I'm exhausted on one level and totally energized on another. I've spent the last two hours reading through the notes that everyone's been taking.

Peter wanders over and pulls up a seat next to me.

"So anything jumping out at you yet?"

"Not yet. How about you?"

"Me neither. But the good news is that I'm getting that small, tickly feeling in the back of my mind. Means something's close."

"I've had that feeling for the last few days. But whatever it is that's trying to break through is sure taking its sweet time."

"It'll come."

Jimmy comes in with coffee and platters of eggs, bacon,

and toast. Miriam wanders in yawning and muttering something about smelling coffee.

And just in time for the food, Marissa and Jeremy clomp up the steps.

We enjoy the camaraderie of a team enjoying a meal together. Then we plan out the day.

Miriam says she's going to call in sick. She's having too much fun, and no one will even notice that she's gone. Everyone claps.

Marisa and Jeremy are going to keep plugging away on the videos and help Miriam go through the research.

I've got to get back to my real job for a few hours. So does Dave.

Peter is going to go back to the hotel, sleep for a few hours, and then come back.

I realize that I've got some extra clothes with me from my trip, so I head back to the hotel with Peter to shower and change.

We get outside, and the fresh air feels good.

"This is my last day. I'm running out of time."

"Yup. You are. This is what I used to call the witching hour. You've got this huge stewpot of ideas and facts and impressions, and it's all turning around and bubbling in your brain. The one thing I learned was to never rush it."

"You're not helping."

He laughs and pats me on the back.

"What did you do when the ideas just didn't come?"

"It never happened. There were times when the ideas came when I stood up in front of the client. No storyboards or print mock-ups—no visual aids at all. That actually only happened once."

"Did you pull it off?"

"One of the best presentations I ever made."

"Did you guys ever lose?"

"All the time. But it was usually because the client was

too chicken to take the kind of risks we would propose. And sometimes they were probably right. But we never wanted to play it safe. It wasn't our style."

We walk.

"What is that stewpot saying to you right now, Ryan?"

"It's mostly just voices. Lots and lots of voices. Of all the wonderful, kooky people I've met in the last week."

"What are they saying?"

"That Leary just isn't cool anymore."

"Too obvious. We know that. Leary knows that. That's why they're looking for a big change. What else are they saying?"

I think and think. But I just shake my head.

"They're there, Ryan. They're talking to you. But you're not listening. Just like Leary's not listening."

His eyes twinkle, and then he gives a nod that seems to say we've spoken enough. We head into the hotel.

*   *

When we get up to the room, Ann is asleep. I shower and change in the bathroom. When I come out, she is gone, and Peter is already fast asleep.

Ann is waiting for me in the main room. I take a seat with her at the small dining table, where she's got coffee for both of us.

"I wanted to kill you at first when you showed up at the cabin, but now I want to thank you."

"Thank me?"

"I haven't seen Peter so excited and happy in practically three years."

"I'm glad."

"But we have to be careful. He's much more fragile than he'd have us all believe. He'll burn the candle at both ends until he collapses. I can't let that happen."

"I understand. Whenever you think he's had enough, just let me know, and I won't push it."

My phone keeps buzzing with Tweets coming in.

"You can take that if you need to."

"Actually, it's not someone calling me. It's Tweets from Twitter."

"Ah, Twitter. Do you know that someone set up a 'Where's Peter Vine' account, and it's got over a hundred thousand followers? We have no idea who it is."

"Doesn't surprise me."

"How many people are you following?"

"Oh, I shut most of them off. Got tired of updates about what people were having for lunch and how many times their dog got sick on the rug."

"So who's that?"

I don't answer.

"You're embarrassed. Must be a girlfriend."

"An ex, actually. She's getting married and sharing the entire process. And as much as I want to stop getting them, I can't."

"Do you still love her?"

"Don't waste any time, do you?"

She smiles but doesn't say anything.

"She's from a super wealthy family, and although they liked me, I think her parents were always hoping I was just a fling."

She's like a therapist. Just waits for me to continue.

"An advertising guy, even at one of the best agencies around, wasn't impressive enough for them. And my family isn't exactly off the *Mayflower*."

"Ouch."

"Yeah, ouch. She defied them for quite a while, but she was so torn between us that I just couldn't take it anymore."

"So who broke up with whom?"

"I guess I walked. But it was really her parents who broke

us up. No one should live torn in half like that. If she married me, her parents would have made her miserable and used money to manipulate us. I didn't want to live like that."

"How long ago was this?"

"Two years."

"Still hurts, huh?"

"I guess I'm still wondering if I should have stuck it out. Love conquers all and all that."

"It can conquer a lot, but it's also messy. One of the best parts of my marriage is the relationship I have with my in-laws. They love me to pieces, and that means so much."

"So maybe I did the right thing?"

"Messy."

"Yeah, messy. And pathetic. Hanging on by a Tweet."

She smiles. She's so cool. Peter's a lucky man. I wave and head out.

*   *

I glance through the Tweets as I wander toward H&V.
Hate the dress. Hate the dress. Hate the dress.
What to do? What to do? What to do?
Ideas? Help. Help. Help. Ahhhhh!

I get to my desk and boot up. What to deal with first— Voice mail? E-mail? Texts? Cell voice mail? And there go the IMs as well.

Two voice mails. The trolls telling me I have a meeting with them at 1:00 tomorrow afternoon. The bitch asking me to call.

Only twenty e-mails. Ten are junk. Delete, delete, delete. A few from the Olsen twins asking for media budgets and project plans. One from Nate telling me to stop by when I get a chance. One from last night from Chas confirming the shoot. Oh yeah. The shoot. Guess I should be there. Oh well.

Cell voice mails are more interesting. Rach wanting to

know how things went last night. Ramon asking me to give a call. Kristina (finally) asking, "Who is Ryan who answers your phone, and when is my audition?"

One from Esther asking how things are going. Gotta call her back right away.

On to texts. Delores from yesterday curious as to what's going on. Four from Kristina. Poor Dave from the shoot saying it's going tolerably well and that it's fun watching Chas sucking up to his girlfriend.

I call Esther and thank her profusely and give her a quick update. She tells me to keep the car as long as I need to and not to worry.

I also call and thank Delores and tell her I can't say too much right now, and she understands. She tells me that Jack hated the pitch but is at a loss as to what to do.

I call the bitch. We touch base on business. I lie as usual and tell her the final art for the ads is coming along fine.

Then she gets excited and tells me that Don has totally changed his tune and has been treating her like gold, and yes, he's coming up to New York this weekend! What should they do? Where should they eat? What should she wear? Should she let him stay at her place? Should he get a hotel room?

This is too hilarious. She's a thirty-one-year-old woman, and she's acting like a teenager. I spend a half hour planning out the whole weekend for her, including sending her an e-mail with links and ideas.

Then I'm off to Nate's lair. We sit together and have a cup of horrible coffee, and he gives me the background on the exchanges between our lovebirds. I ask him if he's done any real work in the last week, and he just laughs and says he hasn't done any real work for three years.

I go back to my cube and call Ramon. He asks me how it's going, and I tell him. When I get to the end, I admit that, for as much work as we've done, I haven't had the breakthrough we need. He tells me to hang tough and that he wants to show me something. He'll stop by Jimmy's this evening.

I plow through some real work. Figure I better get the budget summary to the trolls. Then I tackle the media budgets and project plans for the Flake-Off twins and get those off.

Bruce stops by, and we chat about the Thursday meeting. He asks if I want him to be there. I tell him that I'll be okay, that it's probably better for him if I go alone. He tells me that the trolls have asked for an interim review of my performance, and that he bent over backward to say that I've turned around an impossible account and that the client loves me. I thank him.

I head back to my cube, and there's Rach. She makes me smile, despite all my burdens.

"Hey, you."

"Hey, you. What's doing?"

"Drew has us all in a tizzy making changes and more changes."

"Anything getting better?"

"They're not getting better or worse. I think he's just nervous. Making changes gives him something to do so that he doesn't have to do what he should be doing."

"Yeah, like starting over."

"Exactly. How are you doing?"

"I can't even answer. I don't know. I'm thrilled with all the help I'm getting. I'm amazed. And spending time with Peter is so cool. But I'm scared. Something is blocking me, and I don't know what it is. I feel like the answer is right in front of my face and I just can't see it. And this is it. I'm out of time."

"Tell me what Peter has said to you."

"He keeps telling me to listen to what all the people I've spoken to are saying. He said I'm not really listening. Just like Leary isn't listening."

"He sounds like a Zen master."

"Yeah, exactly. Sometimes I think he already knows the

answer, but he won't tell me because I have to figure it out for myself."

"I don't think he'd do that. I think he's trying to guide you, but it's not his pitch, it's yours."

"How did we get ourselves into this?"

"I keep asking myself that. But I'm glad we did. At least we feel like we're trying."

"Let's see what the word on the street is."

"Oh yeah, by the way, that Janice Stone from *Advertising Weekly* called me again. I told her to call me next week and I'll tell her anything she wants."

I open my browser, and we cruise around to all the marketing rags and then to the real insider sites and blogs.

The general word is that there's no word. Everyone is keeping mum. No leaks. The only thing that is clear is that Leary is seeing all four agencies in one long day and then making an immediate decision. But we already knew this.

"Seems everyone's too nervous to talk. Don't want to get caught and blow their chances."

It's about three o'clock, and I want to get back over to Jimmy's. Rach wants to walk over with me, but she's got to come right back.

We decide to walk a few blocks out of the way so we can keep talking. I tell her that Ramon is stopping by later. She says she'll try to be there.

"Listen, Ry, I wanted to let you know that I really did have a great time on Saturday at Paul's."

"Me, too. Sorry I got carried away and blew it."

"You didn't blow it, Ryan. You're my best friend in the whole world, and I couldn't stand it if something like going out or having sex messed up things between us."

This is not exactly what I want to hear. I'd be more than happy to mess things up.

She takes my arm, and we just walk a few blocks together

without talking, which is fine. I'm happy to just have her on my arm.

*   *

Rach takes off when we get to Jimmy's; she's already late and has to get back. I go in and head on up to the war room, where things are buzzing. Peter looks up when I come in.

"Ah, there you are."

He nods me toward a separate table where he and Miriam have a relatively smaller stack of research binders.

"We've all spent the day going back over everything, and we've isolated what we think are the more important facts and observations. The Post-its mark pages where there are particularly interesting items. And Miriam took another stab at a summary, now that she's had a chance to really dig in."

Miriam hands me a three-page document.

"Listen, Ryan, there's a lot of solid stuff in here. I've got to get going, but I want to thank you for letting me in on this little adventure. I had more fun last night and today than I've had since Peter left. I wish I was the one who could help you through the next step, but that was always Peter's thing."

She hugs me.

"Good luck, Ryan, and call me if you have any questions."

Jimmy walks her out. Hmm. Interesting.

Peter is staring at me.

"Ryan, I've got to go, too. Too much excitement and who knows what will happen. Esther is going to drive us back up to Stockbridge. I figured you guys could use a crash pad close by, so I paid for the hotel room for another night."

He hands me the key cards.

"Wow, I really appreciate that. And everything. You've done more than you know."

"And you've done more than *you* know."

He and Ann both hug me.

"Good luck, everyone. Walk out with us, Ryan."

We walk down and out front, where Esther is waiting with the Charger. She comes over and hugs me and then hands me a huge Tupperware container of cookies—peanut butter, oatmeal, and chocolate chip.

Peter tries to open it, and Esther slaps his hand.

"There's plenty in the car for you. Those are for the team."

Esther gets behind the wheel, and Ann gets in the back. Peter shakes my hand.

"You're close, Ryan. It'll happen. I promise."

He gets in, and with a wave, they take off.

I head back in, wishing I was as confident as he is.

*   *

When I get back upstairs, Marissa runs me through the video collage she's put together. She's put some great music behind it, and I have to say it's quite impactful in making the case for Leary's declining market share.

She's really done a great job. She then shows me the other piece that she's put together. It's the same group of people— Ramon, the high school kids, Dougie, the models—all talking about why fashion is so important to them. Again, it's only a few minutes long, but it packs a nice wallop.

I then spend some more quality time with the culled-down research and Miriam's summary.

Then I put my head down on the table and take a nap. I've been up for thirty-six hours.

*   *

I wake up because Ramon is shaking me. I come to slowly. It's 7:00 PM, and everyone is here.

Jimmy comes in and hands me a cup of coffee.

Ramon lets me wake up and then gives me a toned-down version of his bump and grind. I'm feeling better, even with just two hours of sleep.

I can tell that Ramon wants to speak in private. We head downstairs and make our way to the back of the pub, where it's not too crowded. We sit in a booth, which gives us a modicum of privacy.

We chat a bit, and Ramon gets a good laugh out of Kristina's ruthless persistence. We agree that we like her, even if she's not necessarily the brightest bulb on the porch. She has other attributes to be appreciated.

Ramon finally gets down to business, and I can tell he's a bit uncomfortable. He has a black portfolio with him, and he opens it up.

"Listen, Ry, I haven't shown this stuff to anyone before. Only my moms. She's the only one."

I don't say anything. I really can't say anything because I have no idea what he's going to show me.

He takes out four sheets of paper and spreads them out on the table before me. They're drawings of women's dresses. Now I'm no expert, but they're absolutely stunning. The lines are amazing, and the colors are incredibly dramatic. My mouth falls open a bit, and now I really don't know what to say.

"You did these?"

He shakes his head. He's looking at me expectantly. I realize that, like any artist or writer or creator of anything, he is holding his breath in anticipation of how I'll react. I'm the first one he's decided to share his work with, and as such, he's given me an enormous power and responsibility. If I react the wrong way, he may never draw again, this despite his cool, tough guy exterior.

"These are stunning, Ramon."

I don't qualify it or say I don't know anything about woman's fashion. I leave it at that. All I know is that I'd love to see them on Rach. That's the main thought that goes through my mind, and it's enough.

"Really?"

"Really."

"I've got more."

He shows me about fifteen more drawings, all women's dresses, and they're all amazing.

"Why haven't you shown these to anyone?"

"Too scared."

"You?"

"I got a reputation to keep up."

"You're right. Everyone knows only gay guys design women's dresses."

"You laugh."

"So what are you going to do? Keep them hidden in that portfolio bag forever? You know everyone in the entire business. You could get them looked at anywhere you want."

"That's where you're wrong. That's not how it works. I'm cool, I got some juice, I have a rep for getting things done that can't get done. But it's all on the underside. We're the ones that get shit done behind the scenes. But that's our place. Behind the scenes. They'll never listen to me. Say I try to move forward, cross that line, and I get shot down—then I lose everything. My street cred will be gone. I'll be just another wannabee designer running around with a portfolio."

"It means a lot to me that you trusted me with this. It really does. And all I can say is don't stop. You're talented. Very talented. And I'll help you in any way I can."

"Cool."

We both stand and do that hug thing that guys do, where we mostly slap each other on the back. I can't resist.

"You faggot."

We burst out laughing and head upstairs to join the others.

*   *

It's getting late, and everyone's still tired from last night, not to mention the whole week. At about eleven I give one of the hotel keys to Marissa, and she, Jeremy, and Dave head out to crash at the hotel. Ramon heads out as well. There's not much more they can do anyway. It's up to me now.

I'm actually kinda glad when they're all gone. Especially at this point, when they all keep looking at me expectantly. I need some alone time.

Pitch Day—Thursday

It's just past midnight. I surround myself with the research on one side and the stuff that Marissa has created on the other. I'm at her workstation, so I can look at the videos she's created.

It's quite impressive what we have, given that we have no overarching concept. That's a bit of an inside joke. There are times when you have to just keep moving forward. But it's always better when you have the idea first. Duh.

Jimmy comes in, puts a cup of coffee in front of me, and silently walks out again.

I watch Marissa's video montages again. They really are great. And then for some reason I click into her source files and start watching all of the videos we shot, from beginning to end.

I'm looking for consistencies, times when they all say the same things. Then I swing around and grab Miriam's summary. I remember something. Yes, there it is on her second page.

It clicks off a connection somewhere deep in my synapses. It's what Peter said. "You're not listening to them. Neither is Leary." And then Ramon. "They'll never listen to me."

I go back to the original piece of research—some of the more recent focus groups that were done the prior year.

There it is again. I mark the page with a blue Post-it instead of Miriam's yellow. Then I'm flipping back to some of the other research, the brand research from just a few months ago.

And there it is again. Another blue Post-it.

Tumblers are starting to fall into place in my mind.

The next several hours are a blur. I'm in the zone. Finally, finally, finally. The fatigue is gone.

I go back to the videos. Marissa has laid down time code, so I mark the in and out numbers of the clips I need on a pad. Then I order them the way I want them.

My argument is coming together. And then another big tumbler slides into position. I'm going to have to get Ramon back here first thing in the morning. With his designs. And Marissa is going to have to shoot him.

I write up an outline of what questions to ask him so he'll say what I need.

Then I jump back onto the computer and start writing some PowerPoint slides. I've also got the earlier ones made by Marissa and Jeremy.

Time has flown. It's already 5:00 AM. I'm going to have to wake up Marissa soon and get Dave over here to help set up the shoot.

I'm suddenly starving. Who knows why, but a big, furry blue image jumps into my mind and says, "Cookie!" I do my best Cookie Monster imitation as I devour two of each kind of cookie.

The sugar rush helps.

One more big piece needs to get done. This concept is going to require a huge online effort. Probably more of the budget than the advertising itself. I've got to come up with some really nice mock-ups of what an overall Web site will look like and then a whole bunch of supporting promotional sites as well.

I start drawing out what I'll need on flip charts.

It's 7:00 AM.

I grab my phone and call Marissa. She says she'll jump in the shower and be over in thirty minutes at the most. "Should I bring Jeremy?"

"Yes. That kid can do anything. And get Dave up when you're ready to leave and tell him to go borrow the lighting stuff we used the other day."

I keep going on the Web site pages.

Marissa walks in around seven thirty. I show her what I need, and she gets right on the video editing without asking any questions. She gets it.

Jeremy walks in a half hour later, and I go over the Web stuff. He asks a few questions and then fires up Photoshop on his machine and gets to work. He's got to bang out like twenty page mock-ups in the next several hours. I tell him to make them into jpegs and bring them into PowerPoint slides. He gets it.

I call Ramon and wake him up. I tell him I need him to get his ass back here as soon as he can, and to bring his designs. He hears the tone of my voice and doesn't ask any questions. He says he'll be there within the hour.

Jimmy, my hero, shows up with breakfast for all of us, sees the look on my face, smiles, and disappears.

Before I take off, I go over the interview questions for Ramon with Marissa. I also tell her that she'll have to mount Ramon's designs on presentation boards—as big as possible. She says there's a Staples around the corner where she can get everything she needs. I hug her.

Now there's one more thing I have to take care of—and I finally know exactly how I'm going to do it.

I head to H&V.

*　　　*

I head right back to talk to Nate. I ask him if he can mount a few webcams in the conference room. He says sure. I tell him that I'd like to be able to broadcast the presentation onto a private Web address. And I don't want anyone in the room to know. Then I ask him to take a walk with me around the corner.

I explain everything to him. The whole plan. I take him over to Jimmy's and show him the war room. He knows Marissa and Dave, and I introduce him to Jeremy. I don't have time to run him through the whole presentation, but he just stands there smiling.

Then we walk back together, and I tell him what I need him to do. He doesn't like it. But he gets it. He's in. He's excited. We head back.

It's 9:00 AM.

*   *

Rach calls me as soon as I get to my desk.

"Hey."

"Hey. You okay?"

"Yes. We're getting there. Listen, I can't explain everything right now, but it's going to happen. Just trust me and don't worry. How are you?"

"I'm dressed funky, with lots of leg and cleavage showing, and Drew is pacing around driving us all crazy."

"I gotta run."

"Bye."

I click off.

My phone rings. It's the bitch. I pick up.

"Hey, Rebecca."

"Hey, Ry."

"How ya feeling? You excited?"

"I'm excited and scared. And listen, thanks for all your help."

If she only knew.

"No problem. You okay with the schedule?"

We end up chatting for a half hour. I give her all the time she needs.

By the time I get off, it's 10:00 AM.

I head back to see Nate again. We spend an hour together going over the plan.

*   *

It's 11:00 AM when I head back to Jimmy's.

Marisa shows me the video of Ramon. She's done it perfectly. We edit it together for a half hour.

The boards with Ramon's designs look great. We cut it down to the ten best ones.

Another synapse fires off in my brain.

Hate the dress. Hate the dress. Hate the dress.
Help. Help. Help.

I send my ex a private message and tell her to call Ramon. I text Ramon and tell him she might call.

I then spend the next forty-five minutes with Jeremy, making adjustments to the Web site mock-ups. In order to get them all done, he's taken a minimalist approach, and it works well enough. I'll have to talk to them as I present, but that's fine. They'll work.

It's now noon. I run over to the hotel for a quick shower but skip the shave. I throw on an old pair of jeans and sneakers and head back to H&V.

I arrive just in time to walk into the trolls' conference room at exactly 1:00.

*   *

I sit and wait. I figure they'll let me stew for a while. I don't care. I check my e-mail while I wait.

The trolls enter at 1:05. They sit on the opposite side of the table. I give them a big smile.

"Hey, guys."

"Mr. Simmons."

"Listen, let's cut to the chase. What's the deal?"

"The deal is you're fired. You really pissed off Drew. We actually took your side. So did Bruce. He totally went to bat for you. But you violated company policy by releasing the creative without approval."

"So that's it then? I'm fired?"

"There's nothing we can do."

"I understand. Is anything going to happen to Chas?"

"No. We can't prove whether the photographer was or is his girlfriend. He denies it."

"All right then. So what do I have to do?"

"Give us your key card. We'll give you an hour to pack up

your stuff and leave the building. Your e-mail has already been turned off. You'll receive a check for two weeks pay and any accrued vacation time."

I give them my key card.

"Is there anything I need to sign?"

"No. You don't have an employment contract. You've always been 'at will.'"

"Well, all right then. Thank you, gentlemen."

I stand and start to leave.

"Ryan?"

"Yeah?"

"We really did go to bat for you. We know that Chas and Drew are total assholes. We wish you the best."

"Thanks, guys. I appreciate it."

I shake their hands and head out.

*   *

I knew it was coming, but I feel like I'm floating. As much as we bitch and moan, H&V has been my home for years. I hate Drew and idiots like Chas, but there are a lot of great people here who I'll miss. I wander back down to my cube in a daze. Bruce is waiting for me. I throw my meager belongings into my backpack.

"I did everything I could, Ryan. I hope you believe that."

"I know you did, Bruce. I knew that this could happen."

We discuss how he'll tell the client. I tell him to try to hold off until Monday. I don't want to ruin her weekend with Don.

"Ryan, I don't understand one thing. Why didn't you use the video? It would have shown that Chas was lying."

I put my hand on Bruce's shoulder and look him in the eye.

"Because a wise old woman once told me, 'Sometimes you have to lose a battle or two in order to win the war.'"

With that, I smile and wink. Then I'm gone.

*   *

As I head over to Jimmy's, I make a phone call.

"Advertising Weekly, how may I direct your call?"

"Janice Stone please."

"One moment."

I'm surprised that she actually picks up.

"This is Janice."

"Janice, hi, you don't know me, but you've been trying to speak to a friend of mine at H&V, Rachel Weiss."

"Okay, I'm listening."

"I'm going to give you some information. Whether or not you use it is up to you."

"Okay."

"Don't ask any questions."

"Okay."

"There's a bar on Forty-eighth Street, between Madison and Fifth Avenue, called Old Towne Bar. The B in bar is missing, so it looks like 'Old Towne Ar.' The bartender's name is Jimmy. He'll be expecting you, and he'll show you where to go. Be there a few minutes before four o'clock."

"Four o'clock is when the H&V pitch starts."

"You are quick."

"You need to tell me what this is about."

"No can do. I've got to go."

I click off.

*   *

It's 2:00.

I get to Jimmy's and tell him about Janice. He says he's seen her picture on advertisingweekly.com, so he knows what she looks like.

I head upstairs. It's time to bring everything together, and I don't have much time. I sit with Marissa at her work station, and we go through everything piece by piece, building a seamless presentation. Normally, this would be done over the course of a few days, but we've got an hour. Marissa's hands fly over her keyboard and mouse as she does her magic.

I get a frantic text from Rach.

Word is out you got fired!!!!!

Nice to see the H&V grapevine is still up and running.

Yes, I did. But I'll be there. Don't worry. Everything is cool.

??????

Trust me.

K. BTW, The Duke is here.

Good. The more the merrier.

Marissa and I go through it one more time, making slight adjustments. Finally, it's done. We did it.

The presentation is too big to fit on a flash drive, so we copy it onto an external drive, which, of course, Marissa already has ready. It goes into my backpack, along with some extra cables and connectors.

I also pack up all five boxes of research, keeping four binders separate.

The time is now 3:00.

I get a text from Nate.

On the way. Login to http://50.331.67.89; pw goryan. Txt 2123435567 Y/N regarding audio.

I give Marissa the info and she logs in. Everyone gathers round and then cheers when they see the conference room.

Nate has done a great job of placing the cameras. One of the other tech guys steps into the room and starts talking—we hear him loud and clear. I text Y to the number Nate gave me. The tech guy gives a thumbs-up to one of the cameras and bolts out.

Suddenly everyone is staring at me. I know what they're

thinking. What are you doing here when the show starts in forty-five minutes?

And then the answer walks into the room. It's Nate. He silently hands me a nicely folded black T-shirt. I take off my shirt and put it on. It's a classic Kiss concert shirt from 1987, almost identical to the one he's wearing. Then he takes off his red baseball cap and solemnly hands it to me. I put it on.

We're the same height. We're dressed identically. People get it immediately, and they all burst into applause. They're all slapping Nate on the back, and he's grinning from ear to ear.

One of his guys, Justin, is there as well with a hand truck, and we load up the research and head out, cheered on by a chorus of good lucks!

*   *

Justin and I go around to the side to the freight elevator. I keep my head down, and Robbie doesn't even give me a second glance. Just as I thought.

He takes us up the freight elevator to 17. Justin goes first, and I follow, keeping my head down. Nobody gives us a second glance.

The conference room is empty, but it's all set. We wheel the research and boards to the back of the room, where the tech station is set up, and hide them under the table. Justin runs me through where everything is, and we do a superfast check of video and sound. He then takes me through the script again, which I had done previously with Nate, and I feel okay. Drew's presentation is thankfully on the more low-tech side.

We then hook up the external drive, and I click through a few slides to make sure that I can access my presentation. Shit! The video won't load.

Justin grabs the mouse from me and starts clicking around so fast his hands are a blur. He mutters something like "Goddamn Macs" under his breath.

"I'm going to have to save these video files in a different format. Don't worry. Should only take a few minutes."

They always say it will only take a few minutes. I try to stay cool. I'm watching the saving bar on the computer and willing it to go faster.

Five minutes later it's done. He goes back to the PowerPoint and it works.

Whew.

We then check to make sure that the remote is working. It is. I'm going to be clicking for Drew, but I'm going to have to click for myself when I get up. Justin shows me that we've even got extra batteries, just in case.

Justin scoots out just as we hear voices approaching.

I text Bruce and tell him to go to Ar.

I remember that I have Peter's cell phone number, so I text him the URL and password as well.

I get a text from Jimmy saying that Janice has arrived.

It's 3:50.

Showtime.

*   *

The voices become the pitch team and the gang from Leary. They enter and mill around and chat and get refreshments from a credenza off to the side.

The Leary group is the same four that were at the show—Annette, Mitchell, the Viper, and Maurice.

From H&V there's Drew, Jack, The Duke, Chas, and Rach. They all make small talk for a few minutes, and I just keep my head down. As I expected, no one pays attention to the help. I may as well be invisible. Perfect.

Rach doesn't look in my direction, as she's too busy doing her job of charming Mitchell—at least Drew got that part right. I'm relieved that I've escaped her notice because she's the one most likely to recognize me, and I'm not sure how she'd react.

After a few minutes, everyone settles down into chairs arranged to give Drew an audience. I'm following the script, so I slowly lower the lights in the room. I can relax a bit now that it's darker.

Drew thanks everyone, says "we appreciate the opportunity," blah, blah, blah. He is a smooth presenter, I'll give him that.

He continues with how excited we all are, and how much thought and energy we've put into this pitch, and how the whole agency is behind it, blah, blah, blah.

He then introduces the team, our very best people, blah, blah, blah.

"So we'll start with what we've determined is the most important observation about your business—the incredible equity that is Leary."

Right on cue, I roll a video. It's nicely done. It goes on for about three minutes on the history of Leary. It goes back in time, showing the origins of the brand, the advertising, the awards. It's all flashy and cut beautifully to music, and in my humble opinion, it totally misses the point.

Mitchell seems to have liked it, but the three others remain fairly stone-faced.

Drew then launches into the meat of his presentation. It's solid but boring as hell, and he doesn't really bring any great insights into the conversation. It goes on for about a half hour, and I'm clicking away with him as if we've practiced for days.

I'm surprised that he stays away from acknowledging the issues Leary is facing. He mentions their declining market share in passing, but he seems afraid of offending them with any bad news. Big mistake, if you ask me.

And now he heads into the ideas for the new campaigns. I've seen them before, but I'm still staggered by them.

The campaigns that they've come up with are an attempt

to maintain the one-hundred-year-old country club feel that they've used for years while trying to modernize it.

I'm cringing while watching it. It can best be described as "Muffy and Buffy and Biff and Chip go visit the ghetto." We've taken them out of the country club and into the real world.

Here they are with their multicolored friends. Here they are at a NASCAR race. And look, here they are building a homeless shelter.

I'm being a bit harsh here, but it really is that bad.

Drew takes them through the print campaign and the storyboards for the television commercials, and then he hits briefly on how they'd upgrade the Web site.

He ends with twenty seconds of video highlights from the opening video, mixed in with the new campaign.

He ends with a flourish, and I slowly bring up the lights. His presentation lasted just about an hour.

Chas starts clapping but quickly stops.

The silence that follows is absolutely stunning. It's the loudest thing I have ever heard in my life.

Finally, Annette speaks up.

"Well, it's been a long day. We asked the four most creative agencies in the world to take nothing for granted and blow us away with new ideas. And all four of you have presented variations on the same old crap we've seen for years. I expected more of you, Drew. I feel like I'm in a bad joke that just keeps getting worse."

The looks on the H&V faces are priceless. I look quickly from Drew to Chas to Duke Owen. They're shocked. Jack, on the other hand, doesn't look surprised at all.

I count to ten slowly and then stand and walk to the front of the room. I take off the baseball cap. Rachel's mouth drops opens in surprise. Then she smiles. And a few blocks away, unbeknownst to me, a huge cheer erupts in the back room of a particular bar-pub thing.

"You're right, Annette. And the good news is that what you just saw is a joke. We presented it on purpose to make it clear how big an issue you're facing."

Drew recognizes me, and his face contorts into a mask of fury. He makes a movement to stop me, but Jack grabs his arm and makes him sit. Duke Owen grabs him from the other side. Chas is livid, glaring at me with daggers shooting out of his eyes, but he doesn't have the guts to do anything.

"Now, let's get down to business, shall we?"

I click through Jeremy's slides.

"You guys are in trouble. There's no way to sugarcoat it. Your sales are down 6, 7, and 8 percent over the last three years. Profits are down an average of 4 percent across every category and brand group. Some are down over 8 percent when looked at individually. Your stock price is down 15 percent over the past few years.

"Let's face it. You're getting knocked around by the other big guys, and cherry-picked by the celebrity designer flavors of the season. They're faster and more nimble, and their costs are lower." I'm clicking through Marissa's competitive slide.

"To put it bluntly, you guys are getting your asses kicked."

I actually see a tiny glimmer of a smile on Annette's lips.

"But the numbers only tell one part of the story. The other part, I'm sorry to say, is even worse. You're not cool anymore. And you've become tone-deaf."

I click and the room fills with sound. As our video comes to life on the screen, we hear from Dougie and Ramon and the models. We hear them talking incredibly candidly about how they used to love and respect Leary, but how, over the past few years, they've become cold and arrogant. They're too slow to pick up on trends. We hear Paul explain his concerns.

It's especially powerful when the models discuss how they don't like it when they have to wear Leary at the shows.

The final blow, though, is the high school kids. The video

ends on their line about how they don't need "that Muffy and Buffy bullshit."

I've certainly got their attention.

I walk to the back of the room and wheel out the hand truck filled with their research. I make my way back to the front of the room.

"Let me tell you what we've been doing these last few weeks. In addition to combing through every scrap of research you sent over, we've been out there getting to know your business. We've been shopping and talking to customers and salesclerks. We've been down in warehouses in the garment district. We've been out at the clubs hanging out with the models. We've been behind the scenes at the shows talking with the stylists and agents.

"And we've been out there talking with the so-called urban youth, who are the true trendsetters. And you saw their opinion.

"The good news is that there's hope. And it's actually right here in your own research. We just had to do a bit of digging."

I grab the top binder off the huge stack, walk over, and hand it to Maurice.

"Maurice, would you be kind enough to open that binder and turn to page 47?"

He looks a bit surprised but does as he's asked.

"Please read out loud the part that's circled. This is from one of your focus groups from last year."

Maurice takes a pair of glasses out of his front pocket and opens the binder. He finds the part and reads out loud.

"Twenty-three-year-old male participant. 'Man, I am so sick and tired of seeing what comes out each year. I really don't need all these uptight fashionistas telling me what to wear. I've got my own style.'"

I take the binder back from him and replace it on the stack. I grab another one and walk over and hand it to Katrina.

"Katrina, same exercise. Please open that binder to page 82 and read the part that's circled. This is from one of your trend studies from 2007."

Katrina seems a bit put out but plays along.

"'The study found that over 71 percent of the respondents stated that they do not like being talked down to by the fashion industry. Even more significant is the fact that the number jumps to over 92 percent among the top 20 percent of purchasers of mid- and high-range clothing and accessories.'"

"Hmmmm. Ninety-two percent."

I grab the binder, return it, and grab a third, which I hand to Mitchell.

"Mitchell, you know the deal. Please turn to page 39 and, yeah, yeah, read the circled part. This is from a brand study last year."

Mitchell, instead of being put off, seems to be enjoying the performance.

"Verbatim from a twenty-eight-year-old woman. 'What I love about this brand is that they have this online questionnaire thing where they ask me what I'd like to see next season. And then they do it.'"

I take the binder back.

"And then they do it. Hmmmm."

I grab one more and hand it to Annette.

"Page 21. This is from an *Advertising Weekly* study from two months ago."

Annette finds it and reads.

"'The largest trend of all for the next five to ten years will be user-generated everything. Marketers who jump on this bandwagon will be around for the next few decades. The others won't.'"

I take back the binder.

"User-generated everything. Interesting."

I click and the screens pop to life again with our various subjects.

We hear again from Dougie, Ramon, and the models—all saying how there are so many voices that aren't being listened to, that all the styles just get crammed down their throats. And then we see the high school kids again, showing the looks and styles that they create for themselves out of whatever they can afford.

The video ends.

"What I'm going to propose to you right now is going to scare the crap out of you. It's going to require much more than just changing your advertising. It means completely changing the way you do business.

"What I'm suggesting is that, over the course of the next several years, you almost completely turn your business over to your customers.

"What do I mean by this? It's quite simple. Use the Internet to conduct massive ongoing competitions that anyone can enter. The technology is there, it's ready."

I pop up the Web site mock-ups. I flip through them, demonstrating how people will participate.

"Instead of introducing a new ad campaign, you issue an announcement. A proclamation. A declaration. A manifesto! You tell the whole world that over the next few years, Leary is transforming its business so that 80 percent of all of its designs will come from anyone, anywhere in the world, who submits his or her design and gets voted the most popular. It will be participatory marketing on a grand scale.

"The other 20 percent will be reserved for the best of the best. There will always be a market for elite designers, and Leary will work with them.

"I'd like to end with one more thing."

I click and the video of Ramon we took this morning rolls. He's in shadow, so you can't see who he is, but his voice comes through.

Meanwhile, I get the boards, and Rachel jumps up to help me show them.

"Hi. I'm an unknown. I'd never be able to get my designs in front of the powers that be at a place like Leary. I wouldn't even get in the building. My stuff would never see the light of day."

I let them look at Ramon's designs for a bit.

Then I click on the lights.

"Thank you."

*   *

Now it's my turn to feel like Ramon did last night. This was my creation, and I wait in judgment. I'm petrified.

I don't have to wait long.

Annette stands and smiles and simply starts clapping. Soon the whole room is applauding.

The next few minutes are a blur, with everyone talking at once and shaking my hand.

Then Annette asks if there's a room they can use for a few minutes, and Jack whisks them off to their own conference room.

Rach is staring at me in disbelief. She comes over and gives my hand a quick squeeze that speaks volumes.

I get a Diet Coke and sit for a minute.

Annette and company come back into the room. I stand as Annette comes over to me and shakes my hand.

"I didn't get your name."

"Ryan. Ryan Simmons."

"Well, Mr. Ryan Simmons, I have something I'd like to say. The House of Leary is proud to announce that Halliday and Vine has won our global account. Welcome aboard and congratulations!"

Everyone is cheering and slapping me on the back.

"There is only one small requirement, which I think you'll like. We insist that you head up the account."

More clapping and cheering. I smile to myself. Drew looks at the floor.

"I do have one question, if you don't mind. Whose idea was this? I'd really like to know."

All eyes are on me. I clear my throat.

"We're a team here, Annette. H&V is a team. We're a family. There are too many people to mention. But the setup? The whole joke thing? There was a true master behind that one, and that was none other than Jack Halliday himself."

*   *

Thinking back on it, I'm not sure why I did it. I guess I felt like I owed it to the man. I loved hearing how he took care of everyone, especially Peter. I saw the way Delores and Esther adored him. Now he could move on. Go out with a bang and retire with the grace and dignity he deserved.

The best part of the day was when I finally got back to Jimmy's. The celebration that followed that night was impossible to describe. The party just kept getting bigger and bigger. Word got out at the agency, and many stopped by. Dougie and Paul and the models showed up. We dragged down the high school kids. Even Momma Oracle showed up with enough pie to feed an army.

And Rachel and I decided that enough was enough, and we broke her rule as many times as we could that weekend.

*   *

Pitch Plus 4—Monday

Needless to say, I had a very interesting meeting with Duke Owen on Monday morning. Leary was dead serious about me running the account, and this created something of an unusual situation, as I was, technically speaking, no longer an employee of H&V. The good Duke wasn't used to having the cards stacked against him.

But the situation was resolved amicably enough. There is something about a $350,000 a year salary plus bonus plus options that will make any man swallow his pride. That and a promise that Marissa would be creative director and Bruce would be in charge of account services.

Nate, of course, got all the money he needed to build one of the most amazing Web sites known to man.

Epilogue

It's been three years now since H&V won the Leary business. The effort launched a year after the pitch, and to say that it was a success would be an understatement. Thousands and thousands of people submitted designs. The press was enormous, and sales took off. The contests are now an ongoing part of their business.

The new campaign saved a great brand from probable extinction and set a new standard for brands in practically every category. "Participatory marketing" became the next big industry buzz phrase, much to my chagrin.

I left H&V two years after the pitch. It was time to try something on my own. I founded my own agency and opened the door with one account—Flake-Off dandruff products. The bitch, now known as Rebecca, got married to Don and is now as happy as can be with one kid and another on the way.

Flake-Off became the number one brand this year, with the introduction of the Flake-Off girl, none other than Kristina herself (smiley, smiley), who roamed the country in search of men needing her hair help. There's talk of her own show on Lifetime. She still calls me Alexi.

I don't know where Drew is. He "resigned" from H&V two months after the big win, and hasn't been heard from since. My best friend, Janice Stone, who became the biggest name in advertising journalism after her inside scoop on the big pitch, wrote a piece about his legacy (or the decided lack thereof).

Ramon was hired on the spot by Leary, and he's now one of the biggest names in women's fashion. He has more dresses on the red carpet than anyone else, not to mention a thriving wedding dress business, derived solely from referrals from my ex. But he spends half his time working with the new designers who strive to win the Leary competitions each year. We meet twice a year at Uptown Momma's—I have the pecan, and he has the cherry.

Chas became famous, or should I say infamous, for the YouTube video of the failed shoot and the fight with his girlfriend. At last count, it had over 5.6 million views and was featured on advertisingweekly.com. I have no idea how the video got posted. I think it's safe to say he'll never work in advertising again.

Jack retired a year after the big win and now spends his time giving speeches and sitting on corporate boards. Nothing like going out with a bang—he's a legend now. Delores still works for him and keeps him out of trouble. He couldn't be happier, and he'll do absolutely anything in the world for me. And best of all, I hear that he and his wife are guests up in the Berkshires a few times a year.

The new agency is downtown in the Village in a funky old building. Esther sits right outside my door, watching over me, and there are always cookies around. Jeremy is my CFO, and Dave produces all of our commercials.

Jimmy sold the bar uptown but retained the name. He reopened just around the corner from my agency, but he still hasn't fixed the B. I hear that Miriam hangs out there quite a bit.

Rach stayed at H&V, so we didn't have to keep breaking her rule. We're getting married next year. And I no longer follow my ex.

The office next to mine has the name Peter Vine on the door. He's hardly ever there, and he takes no salary, but it means the world to him that he can stop by anytime he wants, just to shoot the breeze or help out with ideas.

Feel free to come visit. We're always looking for good people. You can't miss it. The name on the door is Ad Asylum.

*   *

Acknowledgments

A huge thank you to my wife and kids for all of your love and support.

And to my parents for so much.

And to Matt for your unquestioning help.

Thank you to all of you who were kind enough to read the manuscript and provide feedback – Julie, Steve, Rachel, Larry, Israel, Barbara, Betty, Nate, Rich, David, and Kirsten - who made sure I didn't commit too many fashion faux pas.

And to every client, boss, and co-worker I've ever had.

And to the entire team at iUniverse – you guys are great.

And especially to all of you readers - I would love to hear from you – please visit www.danwald.com and let me know your opinion!

Made in the USA
Lexington, KY
25 February 2012